Hjalmar Söderberg

DOCTOR GLAS

Hjalmar Söderberg (1869–1941) was one of the most
distinguished of Scandinavian novelists. He was born
and raised in Stockholm and spent the last twenty-
five years of his life in Copenhagen. After working
as a civil servant, he turned to journalism and even-
tually devoted himself full-time to a literary career.
In addition to novels he wrote short stories and
plays as well as literary criticism and philosophical
works about religion. He has been praised for his
fictional vignettes of Stockholm life and for being a
forerunner in the use of psychoanalytic theory and
stream-of-consciousness in his fiction. Söderberg's
novels include *Confusions, Martin Birck's Youth*, and
The Serious Game; *Doctor Glas* is regarded as his
masterpiece.

DOCTOR GLAS

DOCTOR GLAS

A NOVEL

Hjalmar Söderberg

Translated from the Swedish by
PAUL BRITTEN AUSTIN

Anchor Books

A DIVISION OF RANDOM HOUSE, INC.

NEW YORK

FIRST ANCHOR BOOKS EDITION, AUGUST 2002

Library of Congress Cataloging-in-Publication Data
Söderberg, Hjalmar, 1869–1941
Doctor Glas : a novel / Hjalmar Söderberg ;
translated by Paul Britten Austin ;
with an introduction by Margaret Atwood.
[Doktor Glas. English]
p. cm.
ISBN 978-0-385-72267-4
PT9875.S6 D613 2002
20020664458
CIP

www.anchorbooks.com

INTRODUCTION

*Now I sit at my open window, writing—for whom?
Not for any friend or mistress. Scarcely for myself, even.
I do not read today what I wrote yesterday; nor shall I
read this tomorrow. I write simply so my hand can
move, my thoughts move of their own accord. I write to
kill a sleepless hour. Why can't I sleep? After all, I've
committed no crime.*

Doctor Glas was first published in Sweden in 1905, when
it caused a scandal, largely because of its handling of those
two perennially scandalous items, sex and death. I first
read it in the form of a tattered paperback sent to me by
Swedish friends—a reissue of a 1963 translation, published
to coincide with the film based on it. On the back of my
copy are various well-deserved encomiums from newspaper
reviews: "a masterpiece," "the most remarkable book of the
year," "a book of rare quality, developed with true skill."
Nevertheless, *Doctor Glas* has long been out of print in this
English version. It's a pleasure to welcome it back.

The uproar around *Doctor Glas* stemmed from the per-
ception that it was advocating abortion and euthanasia, and
was perhaps even rationalizing murder. Its protagonist is a
doctor, and he has some strong things to say about the
hypocrisy of his own society concerning these matters.
But Hjalmar Söderberg, its author—already a successful

novelist, playwright, and short-story writer—may have been somewhat taken aback by this, because *Doctor Glas* is not a polemic, not a work of advocacy. Instead it is an elegant, vigorous, and tightly knit psychological study of a complex individual who finds himself at a dangerous but compelling open doorway and can't decide whether or not to go through it, or why he should.

The novel's protagonist, Doctor Tyko Gabriel Glas, is a thirtyish medical man whose journal we read over his shoulder as he composes it. His voice is immediately convincing: intelligent, wistful, opinionated, dissatisfied, by turns rational and irrational, and unnervingly modern. We follow him through his memories, his desires, his opinions of the mores of his social world, his lyrical praises or splenetic denunciations of the weather, his prevarications, his self-denunciations, his boredom, and his yearning. Glas is a romantic idealist turned solitary and sad, and afflicted with *fin-de-siècle* malaise—a compound of fastidious aestheticism, longing for the unobtainable, skepticism concerning the established systems of morality, and disgust with the actual. He would like only beautiful things to exist, but has the sordid forced on him by the nature of his profession. As he himself says, he's the last person on earth who should have been a doctor: it brings him into too much contact with the more unpleasant aspects of human carnality.

What he wants above all is action, a feat to perform which might fit the hero he hopes he may carry around inside him. In romances, such deeds often involve a knight, a troll, and a captive maiden who must be rescued, and this is the sort of situation that fate serves up to Doctor Glas. The troll is a flesh-creepingly loathsome and morally repulsive pastor called Gregorius, whom Glas hates even before he finds he has good reason for his hatred. The maiden in captivity is his young and beautiful wife, Helga, who confides

6

to Doctor Glas that she has married Gregorius out of mistaken religious notions, and can no longer stand his sexual attentions. Divorce is impossible: a "respectable" clergyman convinced of his own righteousness, as the Reverend Gregorius is, would never consent to it. Mrs. Gregorius will be enslaved to this toadstool-faced goblin forever unless Doctor Glas will help her.

Doctor Glas has now been given a chance to prove himself. But will he discover that he is a brave knight, an ordinarily timorous nobody, or just as much of a troll as Gregorius, only a murderous one? He contains within himself the possibilities of all three. His name, too, is threefold. *Tyko* refers to the great Danish astronomer Tycho Brahe, who kept his eyes on the stars, far away from the earthiness of the earth—as Doctor Glas so often does throughout the novel. *Gabriel* is the name of the Angel of the Annunciation, proclaimer of the Holy Birth, who is also credited with being the Destroying Angel, sent to wipe out Sodom and Sennacharib, and thought to be the angel of the Last Judgment as well. Thus it's a good name for a medical practitioner, who holds the keys to life and death, but it's also a good name for Doctor Glas, who must decide whether or not to take judgment into his own hands.

And *Glas* is glass: like the diary form itself, it's a reflecting surface, a mirror in which one sees oneself. It's hard and impermeable, but easily shattered; and, from certain angles, it's transparent. This last quality is one of Glas's complaints: he can only fall in love with women who are in love with someone else, because their love makes them radiant; but their love for other men means that Glas himself is invisible to them. So it is with Mrs. Gregorius: she is having an adulterous affair with another man, and can't "see" Doctor Glas. She can only see through him, making of him a means to the end she longs for. As for Doctor Glas's nemesis, it's worth noting that although "Gregorius" is the name of a saint and of a couple of popes, it's also the name of a certain kind of telescope. Like Glas, Gregorius is glassy; he wears glasses, and looking into them, Glas sees the reflection of his own bespectacled self. Perhaps he hates Gregorius so much because the man unconsciously reminds Glas of the father who used to punish him, and whose physicality repelled him as a young boy; or perhaps it's because Gregorius is his ogreish double, the sly, whining, selfish, and self-justifying personification of the lust he can't permit himself to act out.

At first glance the structure of *Doctor Glas* is disarmingly casual, almost random. The device of the diary allows us to follow events as they unfold, but allows us also to listen in on Glas's reactions to them. The workings of the novel are so subtle that the reader doesn't notice at first that it has any: so immediate, even blunt, is the voice that we appear to be reading the uncensored thoughts of a real person. Glas promises candor: he won't set down everything, he says, but he will record nothing that isn't true. "Anyway," he adds, "I can't exorcise my soul's wretchedness—if it is wretched—by telling lies." Chance encounters and trivial conversations alternate with fits of midnight scribbling; jokes and pleasant convivial meals are followed by hours of anguish; night and dreamtime counterpoint the world of purposeful daylight. Unanswered questions punctuate the text—"By the way, why do the clergy always go into church by a back door?"—as do odd moments of hilarity verging on the burlesque, as when Gregorius considers administering the communion wine in the form of pills, to avoid germs. (The pill idea soon recurs in a much more evil form.)

Söderberg had read his Dostoevsky: he too is interested in the disgruntlements of underground men, and in charting impulse and rationalization and motive, and in the fine line that runs between the violent thought and the criminal act. He'd read his ghost-ridden Ibsen and that master of bizarre obsession, Poe. He'd also read his Freud, and he knows how to make use of the semiconscious motif, the groundswells of the unspoken. There are two hints in the text that point us toward the book's methods: Glas's meditation on the nature of the artist, who to him is not an originator but an aeolean harp, who makes music only because the winds of his own time play over him—thus the discursiveness; and his invocation of Wagner, who used the *leitmotif* to connect large swathes of disparate music into a unified whole. A tracing of all the red roses—from dead mother to out-of-reach beloved to rejected potential sweetheart—reveals some of these interconnections, as does a survey of all the astronomical images, from moon to stars to sun to the sunny, starry-eyed Mrs. Gregorius. "Truth is like the sun," says Glas's friend Markel, "its value wholly depends upon our being at a correct distance away from it." And so it would be, we suspect, with Mrs. Gregorius: she can be valuable for Glas as an ideal only as long as she is kept at a correct distance.

Doctor Glas is deeply unsettling, in the way certain dreams are—or, no coincidence, certain films by Bergman, who must have read it. The eerie blue northern nights of midsummer combined with an unexplained anxiety, the nameless Kirkegaardean dread that strikes Glas at the most ordinary of moments, the juxtaposition of pale spirituality with an almost comic vulgar sensuality—these are from the same cultural context. The novel launches itself from the ground of naturalism set in place by French writers of the nineteenth century, but goes beyond it. Some of Söderberg's techniques—the mix of styles, the collage-like snippets—anticipate, for instance, *Ulysses*. Some of his images anticipate the Surrealists: the disturbing dreams with their ambiguous female figures, the sinister use of flowers, the glasses with no eyes behind them, the handless watchcase in which Doctor Glas carries around his little cyanide pills. A few decades earlier and this novel would never have been published; a few years later and it would have been dubbed a forerunner of the stream-of-consciousness technique.

Doctor Glas is one of those marvelous books that appears as fresh and vivid now as on the day it was published. As the English writer William Sansom has said, "in most of its writing and much of the frankness of its thought, it might have been written tomorrow." It occurs on the cusp of the nineteenth and the twentieth centuries, but it opens doors the novel has been opening ever since.

Margaret Atwood

DOCTOR GLAS

I've never known such a summer. A sultry heat-wave since mid-May. All day a thick cloud of dust hangs unmoving over streets and market-places.

Only as evening falls do one's spirits revive a trifle. I am just back from my evening stroll, which I take almost daily after visiting my patients, and they aren't many now in the summertime. From the east comes a steady cool breeze. The heat-wave lifts and drifting slowly off turns to a long veil of red, away to westward. No clatter, now, of workmen's carts; only, from time to time, a cab or tram clanging its bell. My footsteps take me slowly down the street. Now and then I fall in with an acquaintance and for a while we stand chatting at a street corner. But why, of all people, must I keep running into the Rev. Gregorius? I never see that man without remembering an anecdote I once heard told of Schopenhauer. One evening the austere philosopher was sitting, alone as usual, in a corner of his café, when the door opens and in comes a person of disagreeable mien. His features distorted with disgust and horror Schopenhauer gives him one look, leaps up, and begins thumping him over the head with his stick. All this, merely on account of his appearance!

Well, I'm not Schopenhauer. When I saw the parson coming towards me in the distance across the Vasa Bridge I halted abruptly and, turning, leaned my arms on the parapet to admire the view. Grey houses on Helgeand Island. The crumbling wooden architecture of the old Nordic-style bath-house, reflected in The Stream, in whose flowing waters the grand old willows trail their leaves. I hoped the clergyman hadn't seen me, or wouldn't recognise my rear-view. Indeed, I'd almost forgotten him, when suddenly I realised he was standing beside me, his arms like mine resting on the parapet and his head cocked a little to one side—exactly the same pose as twenty years ago, in Jacob's Church, when I used to sit in the family pew beside my late lamented mother, and first saw that odious physiognomy, like a nasty fungus, hop up in the pulpit and heard him strike up with his Abba Father. Same greyish pudgy face; same dirty yellow side-whiskers, now greying slightly, perhaps: and that same unfathomably mean look behind the spectacles. Impossible to escape! I'm his doctor now, as I am many others'. And sometimes he comes to me with his aches and pains.—Well, well . . . good evening, Vicar, And how are you?—Not too good; in fact not at all well. My heart's bad, thumps irregularly, sometimes stops at nights, so it seems to me.—Glad to hear it, I thought. For all I care you can die, you old rascal, and rid me of the sight of you. Besides, you've got a pretty young wife, whom you're probably plagueing the life out of, and when you die she'll remarry and get herself a much better husband. But aloud I said: Really? Really? That so? Perhaps you'd better come and see me one of these days. We'll look into the matter. But there was a lot more than this he wanted to talk about. Important things: It's quite simply unnatural, this heat. And: It's stupid, building great big parliament buildings on that little island. And: My wife isn't really well, either, if it comes to that.

In the end he cleared off, and I went on my way. Entering the Old Town, along Storkyrkobrinken, I strayed among its narrow alleys. A close evening atmosphere among the cramped passages and between the houses: and along the walls strange shadows. Shadows never seen in our quarters.

Mrs Gregorius, yes! That was a queer visit she paid me the other day. She came to my surgery hour. I noticed clearly when she arrived, but although she had come in good time she waited until the last, letting others who had come after her see me first. At last she came in. Blushed and stammered. Finally blurted out something about having a sore throat. Well, it was better now.—I'll come back tomorrow, she said. Just now I'm in such a hurry. . . .

So far she hasn't come back.

Emerging from the alleyways, I walked down Skeppsbron Quay. Over Skeppsholmen Island the moon hovered, lemon yellow in the blue twilight. But my quiet and peaceful mood was gone. Meeting the parson had spoilt it. That there should be such people in the world! Who hasn't heard the old conundrum, so often debated when two or three poor devils are sitting round a café table: If, by pressing a button in the wall, or by a mere act of will, you could murder a Chinese mandarin and inherit his riches—would you do it? This problem I've never bothered my head to find an answer to, perhaps because I've never known the cruel misery of being really and truly poor. But if, by pressing a button in the wall, I could kill that clergyman, I do believe I should do it.

As I went on homewards through the pale unnatural twilight the heat seemed as oppressive as at high noon; and the red dust-clouds which lay in strata beyond Kungsholmen's factory chimneys, turning to darkness, resembled slumbering disasters. With long slow steps I went down past Klara Church, hat in hand, sweat breaking out on my forehead. Not even beneath the great trees in the churchyard was the air cool. Yet almost every bench had its whispering couple; and some, with drunken eyes, sat in each other's laps, kissing.

*   *   *

Now I sit at my open window, writing—for whom? Not for any friend or mistress. Scarcely for myself, even. I do not read today what I wrote yesterday; nor shall I read this tomorrow. I write simply so my hand can move, my thoughts move of their own accord. I write to kill a sleepless hour. Why can't I sleep? After all, I've committed no crime.

*   *   *

What I set down on these pages isn't a confession. To whom should I confess? Nor do I tell the whole truth about myself, only what it pleases me to relate, but nothing that isn't true. Anyway, I can't exorcise my soul's wretchedness—if it is wretched—by telling lies.

*   *   *

Outside, the great blue night hangs over the churchyard and its trees. Such silence now reigns in the town that sighings and whisperings among the shadows down there reach up to me in my eyrie. And, once, an impudent laugh pierces the darkness. I feel as if at this moment no one in the world is lonelier than I—I, Tyko Gabriel Glas, doctor of medicine, who at times help others, but have never been able to help myself, and who, at past thirty years of age, have never been near a woman.

*   *   *

June 14

What a profession! How can it have come about that, out of all possible trades, I should have chosen the one which suits me least? A doctor must be one of two things: either a philanthropist, or else avid for honours. True, I once thought I was both.

Again a poor woman was here, weeping and begging me to help her, a woman I've known for years. Married to a minor official, four thousand crowns a year or so, with three children. In the first three years the babies came, one after another. Since then, for five years, perhaps six, she has been spared. Has regained a little health, strength, youth. She has had time to put her home in order, recuperate a little after all her troubles. Bread, of course, has been short. But they seem to have managed somehow.—And now, all of a sudden, here it is again.

She could hardly speak for tears.

I replied, of course, with my usual lesson. Known by rote, I always recite it on such occasions: My duty as a doctor. Respect for life, even the frailest.

I was serious, immovable. In the end she had to go away; ashamed, bewildered, helpless.

I made a note of the case. The eighteenth in my practice. And I'm not a gynæcologist.

I shall never forget the first. A young girl, twenty-two or so; a big, dark-haired, rather vulgar young beauty, the sort, you could see at a glance, which must have filled the earth in Luther's day, if he was right when he wrote: It is as impossible for a woman to live without a man, as for a man to bite off his own nose. Thick middle-class blood. Father a wealthy business-man. I was the family doctor, so she came to me. She was distraught, out of her wits; but not particularly shy.

—Save me, she begged, save me. I replied with duty, etc., but that was clearly something she did not understand. I explained to her how the Law does not connive at any jiggery-pokery in such cases.—A glance of non-comprehension. The Law? I advised her to confide in her mother: She'll talk to Papa, and there'll be a wedding.—Oh, no, my fiancé hasn't a penny, and Father would never forgive me. They weren't engaged, of course; she used the word 'fiancé' because she could find no other, and 'lover' is a novelist's word, foul in the mouth.—Save me! Haven't you any mercy? I don't know what I'll do! I'll throw myself into the harbour!

I became rather impatient. Indeed, she did not inspire me with any very merciful feelings. These things always arrange themselves, where there is money. Only pride has to suffer a little. She sniffed, blew her nose, talked wildly and in the end threw herself on the floor, kicking and screaming.

Well, in the end it all turned out, of course, as I expected. Her father, a crude blighter, smacked her face once or twice, married her off double-quick to her partner in crime, and packed them off abroad on a honeymoon.

Such cases never worry me. But I was truly sorry for this poor little woman today. So much suffering and misery, for so little pleasure.

Respect for human life—what is it in my mouth but low hypocrisy? What else can it ever be on the lips of anyone who has ever whiled away an idle hour in thought? Human life, it swarms around us on every hand. And as for the lives of faraway, unseen people, no one has ever cared a fig for them. Everyone shows this by his actions, except perhaps a few more than usually idiotic philanthropists. All governments and parliaments on earth proclaim it.

And duty! An admirable screen to creep behind when we wish to avoid doing what ought to be done.

Besides, no one can risk his all, social position, respectability, future, everything, merely to help strangers he is indifferent to. Rely on their silence? That would be childish. Some woman friend gets into the same fix, a word is whispered as to where help is to be found; and soon you're a marked man. No, best stick to duty, even if it is nothing but a piece of painted scenery, like Potemkin's villages. I am only afraid I recite my duty-formula so often that in the end I shall come to believe it. Potemkin only deceived his empress; how much more despicable to deceive oneself.

* * *

Position, respectability, future. As if I were not ready, any day or moment, to stow these packages aboard the first ship to come sailing by laden with action.

* * *

Again I sit at my window. The blue night is awake beneath me; under the trees, rustlings and whisperings.

Yesterday, while taking my evening stroll, my eye fell on a married couple. I recognised her at once. It is not so many years since I danced with her at a ball, and I haven't forgotten how, every time I saw her, she presented me with a sleepless night. But of that she knew nothing. She was not yet a woman. She was a virgin. She was a living dream; man's dream of woman.

Now she goes walking down the street on her husband's arm. More expensively dressed than before, but vulgarly, more the bourgeoise. In her gaze is something extinguished, worn. Yet at the same time it is a contented wifely look, as if she were carrying her stomach before her on a silver-plated salver.

No, I don't understand it. Why must it be like this, why must it always be like this? Why must love be the troll's gold that on the morrow turns to withered leaves, filth, or beery indulgence? Does not all that side of our culture not directly designed to still hunger, or defend us against our enemies, spring from mankind's longing for love? Our love of beauty knows no other source. All art, all poetry, all music has drunk at it. The most insipid modern historical painting, every bit as much as Raphael's madonnas and Steinlen's little Parisian working girls; 'The Angel of Death' as the Song of Songs; and *Das Buch der Lieder*, the Chorale and the Viennese waltz, yes, every plaster ornament on this dreary house I live in, every figure on the wallpaper, the form of the china vase over there, the pattern on my scarf, everything made to delight or embellish—no matter whether successful or unsuccessful—springs from this origin, albeit often by the longest and most circuitous of routes. Nor is this a brainwave of mine, born of the night, but something proven a hundred times over.

But that source's name isn't love. It's the dream of love.

And then, on the other side, everything to do with this dream's fulfilment, instinctual satisfaction, and all that follows therefrom. To our deepest instincts it appears as something ugly, indecent. This can't be proved. It's only a feeling; *my* feeling, and, I believe, everybody's. People always treat each other's love affairs as something low or comic, often not even making exception for their own. And the consequences . . . A pregnant woman is a frightful object. A new-born child is loathsome. A deathbed rarely makes so horrible

20

an impression as childbirth, that terrible symphony of screams and filth and blood.

But first and last, the act itself. I shall never forget as a child under the great chestnut trees in the school-yard hearing a schoolmate explain 'what happens'. I refused to believe it. Several more boys had to come over, laughing at my stupidity, and confirm it. Even then I hardly believed them, but ran away, beside myself with fury. Had Father and Mother done that? And would I do the same, when I grew up? Was there no escape?

Always I had felt a profound scorn for the bad boys who scribbled dirty words on walls and hoardings. But at that moment it seemed to me as if God Himself had scribbled something filthy across the blue spring sky; and I believe it was then I first began to wonder whether God really existed.

Even today I've hardly recovered from my astonishment. Why must the life of our species be preserved and our longing stilled by means of an organ we use several times a day as a drain for impurities; why couldn't it be done by means of some act composed of dignity and beauty, as well as of the highest voluptuousness? An action which could be carried out in church, before the eyes of all, just as well as in darkness and solitude? Or in a temple of roses, in the eye of the sun, to the chanting of choirs and a dance of wedding guests?

*　　*　　*

How long have I been pacing my room? I don't know.

Out there it's becoming lighter, the church cock gleams to the eastward, and the sparrows twitter, shrill and hungry.

Strange, how a shudder always passes through the air just before sunrise.

*   *   *

June 18

Today it has been a little cooler, and for the first time in more than a month I went riding.

What a morning! I had gone to bed early and slept soundly all night. I never sleep without dreaming, but last night's dreams were blue and light. I rode out towards Haga, round the echo temple, past the copper pavilions. Dew and spiders' webs on all the bushes and shrubs, and a great sighing among the trees. Deva was in highest spirits, the earth danced on beneath us, young and fresh as on creation's first Sunday morning. I came to a little inn; having been there often when out for my rides last spring, I recognised it, dismounted, and drained a glass of ale at a gulp. Taking hold of the brown-eyed girl by her waist, I swung her around me; kissed her hair; and rode off.

As the song says.

*   *   *

June 19

So, Mrs Gregorius. And that was her business! Rather unusual, I must admit.

This time she came late, the surgery hour was over, and she was left alone in my waiting-room.

She came in to me, very pale, said 'Good morning' and found herself standing there in the middle of the room. I waved her to a chair, but she just stood where she was.

—I was fooling you last time, she said, I'm not ill; I'm perfectly well. It was something completely different I wanted to talk to you about, Doctor. I just couldn't get it out, then.

Down in the street a brewer's dray went rumbling by. I went over and shut the window, and in the sudden silence I heard her say, in low quick tones, but the words trembling a little, as if on the brink of tears:

—I've conceived such a horrible loathing for my husband.

I stood with my back to the stove, in the corner. I bowed my head, to indicate I had understood.

—Not as a human being, she went on. He's always kind and good to me; he has never said a hard word to me. But he awakens in me such a horrible distaste.

She drew a deep breath.

—I don't know how to express myself. What I thought of asking you is something so unusual. And perhaps it is at variance with what you consider to be right. I don't know what you think of such matters, Doctor. But there's something about you that inspires me with confidence and I don't know anyone else I can confide in in this matter, no one in the whole world who could help me. Doctor, couldn't you talk to my husband? Couldn't you tell him I'm suffering from some disease, some infection of the womb, and that he must give up his rights, at least for a while?

Rights. I passed my hand over my forehead. Every time I hear the word used in that sense, I see red. God in heaven, what has happened to people's brains, that they should have made rights and duties out of it!

It was immediately clear to me that I must come to the rescue here, if I could. But just then I couldn't find anything to say, I wanted her to go on talking. Possibly, too, my sympathy for her was not unmixed with a dose of pure simple curiosity.

—Mrs Gregorius, I said. Forgive me for asking, but how long have you been married?

—Six years.

—And what you call your husband's rights, have they always seemed as difficult to you as they do now?

She blushed a little.

—It's always been difficult, she said. But recently it has become unbearable. I can't stand it any longer, I don't know what will become of me.

—But, I observed, the Vicar isn't a young man any longer. It surprises me that at his age he can . . . bother you so much. How old is he, in point of fact?

—Fifty-six, I think—no, maybe fifty-seven. But he looks older, of course.

—But tell me, Mrs Gregorius—haven't you ever spoken to him about this, yourself? Told him what suffering it is for you, asked him in a simple friendly way to excuse you?

—Yes, I did ask him once. But he answered with a homily. He said we could not know whether God meant to give us a child, even though we haven't had one so far; and that it would therefore be a very big sin if we ceased doing what God wished us to do in order to get a child. . . . And perhaps he's right. But it's so hard for me.

It was more than I could do to suppress a smile. What a hardened old sinner!

She saw me smile, and, I believe, misunderstood it. For a moment she stood there silent, as if gathering her thoughts; then she began speaking again, in a low, trembling voice, while her blush spread higher and redder over her complexion.

—No, she said. You'll have to know the whole story. Perhaps you've already guessed it, you see right through me. I'm asking you to play the fool for my

24

sake. Well then, at least I must be straightforward with you. Judge me as you will. I'm an unfaithful wife. I belong to another man. And that's why it has become so terribly hard for me.

She avoided my glance as she said this. But I,—only now, for the first time, did I really see her. For the first time I saw a woman was standing in my room, a woman whose heart was full of desire and misery, in the flower of her womanhood, perfumed with love, yet blushing with shame that this perfume should be so strong and noticeable.

I felt myself turn pale.

She looked up and met my glance. I don't know what she thought she read in it; but unable to stand any longer, she sank down on a chair, shaken with weeping. Perhaps she thought I was taking the whole matter quite frivolously; or was indifferent and hard, and that she had perhaps exposed herself to a strange man all to no purpose.

I went over to her, took her hand, patted it slowly: There, there, don't cry, don't cry any more now. I'll help you. I promise.

—Thank you, thank you. . . .

She kissed my hand, wetting it with her tears. Another sob. Then a smile shone through her weeping.

I had to smile, too.

—But you were foolish to tell me the last bit, I said. Not because you need be in the least afraid I shall abuse your confidence; but such matters have to be kept secret. Always, without exception, as long as possible! And naturally I should have helped you, anyway.

She answered: —I *wanted* to tell you! I wanted someone I respect and look up to to know about it and yet not despise me.

Then came a long story. Once, about a year ago, she

had heard a conversation between me and her husband, the vicar—he was ill and I was visiting him. Our discussion had turned to prostitution. She remembered everything I had said and now she repeated it to me—something quite simple and ordinary, about these poor girls being human beings, too, and so they ought to be treated as human beings, etc. But she had never heard anyone talk like that before. From that day on she had looked up to me; and that was why she had plucked up courage to come and confide in me.

All this I had totally forgotten. . . . But 'what is lost in the snow comes up in the thaw'.

Well, I promised to talk to her husband that very same day; and she left. But she forgot her gloves and parasol. Coming back to fetch them, she disappeared again, radiant, happy, dizzy with joy, like a child that has got its own way and looks forward to some great pleasure.

*　　*　　*

I went there in the afternoon. She had prepared him, as had been agreed. In a room apart I had a conversation with him. He was even greyer in the face than usual.

—Yes, he said, my wife has already told me how things are. I can't say how sorry I am for her. We had both so deeply hoped and longed for a little child. But I'll have nothing to do with separate bedrooms,—I must make that quite clear. After all, it's so unusual in our circles, it would only lead to gossip. And besides, I'm an old man.

He gave a hollow cough.

—Yes, I said. Of course. I don't doubt that you put your wife's health before everything else, Vicar. And in any case we have good hopes, of course, of getting her well again.

26

—I pray to God we shall, he replied. But how long do you think it may take, Doctor?

—That's hard to say. But half a year's absolute abstinence will certainly be necessary. Then we shall see. . . .

He has a couple of dirty brown spots on his face; they turned even darker and stood out even more clearly, now, against his colourless complexion. It was as if his eyes had shrunk.

*　　　*　　　*

He has been married once before; a pity she died, that first wife! In his study hangs a portrait of her, enlarged from a charcoal sketch; a simple-minded, grumbling, pious, sensual type of lass, not wholly unlike the good Catharine of Bora.

She certainly must have suited him. Pity she died!

*　　　*　　　*

June 21

Who's the lucky man? This question I've been asking myself ever since the day before yesterday.

Odd, that I should so soon get to know the answer. And that it should turn out to be a young man with whom I am acquainted, if only slightly. It's Klas Recke.

Well, well. He's certainly quite another creature from the Rev. Gregorius.

I met them only a little while ago, as I was taking my evening stroll at random through the streets in the warm rose-tinted twilight. I was thinking of her, the little woman. I think of her often. I walked into a deserted side-street—and there, suddenly, I saw them coming towards me. They were just coming out of a doorway. Hastily, to hide my face, I pulled out my handkerchief and blew my nose. It was hardly necessary. He, I am sure, scarcely knows me by sight; and she, blind with happiness, did not see me.

June 22

I sit reading the page I wrote yesterday evening, reading it over and over again, and saying to myself: so that's the way of it, old chap, you've become a pimp, have you?

Nonsense. I've freed her from something horrible. I felt it just had to be done.

What else she does with herself is her own business.

June 23

Midsummer Eve. Light, blue night. From childhood and youth do I not remember you as the lightest, giddiest, airiest of all nights of the year. Why, then, are you now so oppressive, anxious?

I sit at my window, passing my life in review and trying to find a reason why it should have fallen into a furrow so unlike all the others', so far from the highway.

Let me think.

Just now as I crossed the churchyard I saw again one of those scenes of which letters to the newspapers are in the habit of saying they 'defy description'. Obviously an instinct that can compel these wretched people to flout all convention in a churchyard must be an immensely strong and powerful one. It drives frivolous men into all sorts of mad pranks, and forces honest intelligent men to subject themselves to every sort of tribulation and sacrifice. As for women, it drives them to surmount those feelings of modesty which the education of generation upon generation of young girls has been designed to awaken and develop, and causes them

28

to suffer terrible bodily torments and often plunge into deepest misery.

Only me it has so far not driven to anything. How can this be possible? Not until late did my senses awaken and by then my will was already a man's. As a child I was very ambitious, becoming early accustomed to self-control and to distinguish between what was my innermost constant will and transient wishes, the moment's desire. I learned to hearken to the one voice, and despise the other. Since then I have noticed how unusual this is among human beings, more unusual, perhaps, than talent and genius; therefore it sometimes seems to me as though I really ought to have become something unusual, significant. Wasn't I a shining light at school? Always youngest in my class, a student at fifteen, didn't I take my student exam at fifteen and my M.A. at twenty-three? But there I stopped. No special studies followed, no doctor's disputation. There were those who would have been willing enough to lend me money, almost any amount of it; but I was tired. I felt no desire to specialise further. All I wanted was to earn my daily bread. My schoolboy ambition to get high marks, satisfied, had withered away but, oddly enough, no grown man's ambition took its place. This, I fancy, must have been because it was just then I began to think. Up to then I hadn't had the time.

During all those years other instincts had lain half-asleep; they had been enough, certainly, to stir up vague dreams and desires, as in a young girl; but not mighty, imperious, as in other young men. And even if from time to time I lay awake at nights, indulging myself in hot fantasies, yet it always seemed to me un-thinkable that I should find satisfaction with the women my comrades visited, women they had sometimes pointed out to me on the streets, but who to me appeared merely disgusting. This must also have been one reason why my imagination grew so solitarily, almost out of touch with my schoolfellows'. After all, I was so much younger than they were. Therefore when they talked of such things I at first understood nothing; and, understanding nothing, became accustomed not to listen. In this way I remained 'pure', not even making the acquaintance of boyhood sins; scarce knowing what they were. I had no religious faith to sustain me, yet I made up my own dreams of love, oh yes, very beautiful dreams, and one day, I was sure, they would come true. But I had no desire to sully my white student cap or sell my birthright for a mess of pottage.

My dreams of love—once they seemed to me so close, so very close, to realisation! Midsummer night, strange pale night, always you revive that memory which in truth is all I have and which alone remains when everything else sinks away and turns to dusty nothingness. And yet what happened then was so insignificant! I was staying at my uncle's country place during the midsummer holidays. There was youth, and dancing, and games. Among the young people was a girl. I had already met her a few times at family parties, but until then I had not thought much about her. But now when I saw her there, something a schoolmate had once said about her at a party came into my mind: That girl certainly has an eye to you, she's been looking at you the whole evening! Now I recalled this, and although I did not exactly believe it, yet it made me observe her more closely than I might otherwise have done. I noticed, too, that she looked at me from time to time. She was, perhaps, no more beautiful than many another; but she was in the full bloom of her twenty years and over her young breasts she wore a thin white blouse. We danced together a few times round the maypole. Towards midnight we all went up on to a knoll to look out over the wide countryside where a midsummer bonfire was to be lit, our intention being to stay until sunrise. The path led through the forest, between tall straight pines; we went two by two, and I was walking beside her. She stumbled over a root in the shadowy forest and I gave her my hand, and a thrill of pleasure passed through me as I felt her little soft, firm, warm hand in mine. So I went on holding it, even where the path was smooth and easy.

What did we talk about? I don't know, not a word has remained in my memory, all I remember is that a secret current of silent and determined devotion flowed through her voice and all her words, as if this action of walking together with me hand in hand through the forest was something she had long dreamed of and hoped for. We came to the hilltop. The other youngsters, having arrived before us, had already lit the bonfire, and we gathered in groups and scattered couples. Above us the sky hung vast and light and blue; below us lay the creeks and sounds and the deep wide channels, shining like ice as they stretched away into the distance. Still I held her hand in mine, and I believe I also plucked up courage to stroke it slowly. I stole glances at her and saw how her skin seemed to glow in the night's pallor and how her eyes were full of tears, though she wasn't crying, and her breath came quiet and even. Silent, we sat there together. But inside me it was as if I was singing a song, an old song which came to mind, I don't know how:

> *There burns a flame, he burns so clear,*
> *like a thousand wreaths of fire.*
> *Shall I enter that flame with my dearest dear,*
> *and dance with my heart's desire?*

A long while we sat there. Some of the others got up and went off homeward, and I heard someone say: There are some big clouds to the eastward, we shan't see the sunrise. The crowd on the hilltop thinned out, but we two sat on and on, until we were left alone. I looked at her a long while and she met my gaze. Then I took her head between my hands and kissed her, a light innocent kiss. At the same moment someone called her. She gave a little start, tore herself free, and ran away, running on light feet, downwards through the forest.

When I caught up with her she was already with the others and all I could do was silently squeeze her hand, and she pressed mine in response. Down there in the field they were still dancing round the maypole, country girls and farmhands all mixed up with the young gentry, as the custom is on this one night of the year. Again I took her into the dance, a wild and dizzy dance; already it was broad daylight but was the midsummer witchery still in the air; the whole earth danced under us and the other couples flew past, now high above us, now far beneath; everything went up and down, and round and round. So at last we escaped out of the swirling confusion of dancers and, not daring to look at one another, crept away without a word behind a hedge of lilac. There I kissed her again. But now it was something else, her head lay back on my arm, she closed her eyes, and her mouth became a living thing under my kiss. I pressed my hand against her breasts, and I felt her hand lay itself on mine—perhaps she meant to defend herself, or remove my hand, but in fact she only pressed it harder to her breast. Meanwhile a radiance came over her face, faint at first, then stronger, and at last like a violent flash; she opened her eyes, but was forced to close them again, blinded; and when at last we had kissed our long kiss to its end, we stood cheek to cheek, staring amazed straight into the sun which had burst out of the cloud-layers to the east.

I never saw her again. That was ten years ago, ten years ago tonight, and even today when I think of it I feel sick and mad.

We made no tryst next day; it did not occur to us. Her parents lived at a place nearby and we took it for granted we should meet and be together next day, every day, all our lives. But next day it rained and the day passed without my seeing her. And in the evening I had to go into town. A few days later I read in a newspaper she was dead. Drowned while bathing, she and another girl—Yes, it's ten years now, since all that happened.

At first I was in despair. But I must really have quite a strong nature. I worked on, just as I had done before, and took my exam in the autumn. But I suffered too. At nights I always saw her before me. Saw the white body lying among weeds and slime, rising and falling on the water. The eyes were wide open, and open, too, the mouth I kissed. Then people came in a boat with a grapnel. The grapnel fastened its claw in her breast, the same young girlish breast my hand had touched so recently.

A long while was to pass after this before I again felt I was a man or that there were such creatures as women in the world. But by then I was hardened. Once, at least, I had felt a spark from the great golden flame, and I was less than ever inclined to put up with mere dross. Others may be less exigent on that score, that's their business; and I don't know whether the whole question is of much importance. Yet I felt it was important to me, even so. It would surely be naïve to think a man's will could not regulate these trifles, if only the will existed.

Dear Martin Luther, worthy fount of all the Rev. Gregorius' doctrines, what a sinner in the flesh you must have been, and so much nonsense you talked when you came to this chapter! Even so, you were more honest than all your present-day disciples, a fact which shall be held to your credit.

So year followed year, and life passed me by. I saw many women who rekindled my longings, but just these particular women never noticed me. It was as if I did not exist for them.

Why was that?

I think I understand now. A woman in love has just that magic spell about her walk, her complexion, her whole being, which alone can hold me in thrall. And it was always such women who awakened my desires. But naturally, being in love with other men, they did not see me. Instead, there were others who looked at me; after all, I was a qualified doctor of youthful years and with the makings of a good practice. Therefore I was regarded as an excellent match. Indeed, I became the object of a good deal of obtrusive attention. But it was always love's labour lost.

Yes, the years went, and life passed me by. I labour in my calling. People come to me with their maladies, all sorts, and I apply what remedies I can. Some get well, others die, most drag on with their aches and pains. I perform no miracles; one or another whom I have been unable to help has afterwards turned away from me to quacks and notorious charlatans, and got well again. But I think I regard myself as a careful and conscientious doctor. Soon I see myself becoming the typical family doctor, he of the great experience and the calm look that inspires confidence. Perhaps people would not have so much confidence in me if they knew how badly I sleep at nights.

JUNE 28

Midsummer night, pale blue night, once you were so light and airy and intoxicating, why do you lie now like anxiety on my breast?

On my evening stroll yesterday I walked past the Grand Hotel. Klas Recke was sitting at a table on the pavement, alone with his whisky. I went on a few steps, turned, and sat down at a nearby table to observe him. Either he did not see me, or did not wish to. The little woman has naturally told him of her visit to me and its happy outcome—presumably he is grateful for the latter, but perhaps it disturbs him a little to know that there is someone else in the secret too. He sat motionless, looking out over the water, smoking a very long slender cigar.

A newsboy went by; I bought an *Aftonblad* to use as camouflage, observing him over the edge of its page. And the same thought passed through my mind as when I first saw him, many years ago: why has that man got just the face I ought to have had? That is more or less how I would look, if I could re-make myself. I who in those days suffered such torments because I felt as ugly as the devil. Now I don't care.

Hardly ever have I seen a more handsome man. Cold pale grey eyes, but in a frame that makes them dreamy and deep. Perfectly straight and level eyebrows reaching far back toward the temples; a white marble brow, hair dark and rich. But in the lower half of the face the mouth is the only perfectly beautiful feature; otherwise there are small queer features, an irregular nose, a complexion dark and as it were scorched, in a word everything necessary to save him from that sort of flawless beauty which mostly only awakens ridicule.

What does the man look like inside? Of that I know

35

almost nothing. All I know is, he passes for a very clever fellow, seen from the ordinary careerist point of view. I seem to recall having seen him more often in the company of the head of the department where he works, than among his contemporaries.

As I watched him sitting there, motionless, his gaze fixed on abstraction, not touching his glass, and his cigar slowly dying, a hundred thoughts came into my head. A hundred old dreams and fantasies broke out afresh as I thought of the life that is his, and compared it with my own. Often and often have I said to myself: *Desire* is of all things the most delightful, and the only one which in some small degree can gild this miserable life of ours; but the satisfaction of desire can't be much to write home about, judging at least by all these consuls and consuls-general who deny themselves nothing in that line of country and who, even so, have never aroused in me the least qualm of jealousy. But when I see such a man as Recke over there, then, very deep down inside me, I feel bitterly envious. For him that problem which poisoned my youth and which, far though I am advanced in manhood's years, still weighs me down, has solved itself. True, so it has also for most other people, but the solution to the problem causes me no envy, only disgust. Otherwise it would have solved itself for me too. But to him love has seemed from the outset a natural birthright; never has he stood trying to choose between hunger and rotten meat. Nor, I fancy, has he ever had much time for thinking, never had time to let reflection drip its poison into his wine. He is happy. And I envy him.

And with a shiver I thought, too, of her; of Helga Gregorius. Through the twilight I saw that look of hers, quenched in happiness. Yes, these two belong together, it's natural selection. Gregorius! Why must she trail that name and that creature after her through life? It's meaningless.

Night began to fall, a red sunset glow lit up the soot-streaked façade of the Royal Palace, across the water. People passed along the pavement; I listened to their voices. Thin gangling Yankees, with their drawling slang. The nasal tones of little fat Jewish businessmen. And ordinary middle-class folk, a Saturday contentment in their voices. One or another nodded to me; and I nodded back. One or another raised his hat; I raised mine. Some acquaintances sat down at a table quite close to me,—it was Martin Birck and Markel, and a third gentleman I've met some time or other, but whose name I've forgotten or perhaps never known—he's very bald and every time I've met him before it's always been indoors. That was why I didn't recognise him until he took off his hat to greet me. Recke nodded to Markel, whom he knows, and soon afterwards got up to go. Then he passed near my table, saluted me with extreme politeness, if a little distantly. We were on Christian-name terms at Uppsala. But he has forgotten that.

As soon as Recke was out of earshot the company at the table began to discuss him, and I heard the bald gentleman, turning to Markel, ask:

—So you know that chap Recke, he's said to be a fellow with a future—ambitious, they say?

MARKEL:—Yes, ambitious. . . . If I say he's ambitious it's mostly for the sake of our close friendship; otherwise one would be putting the matter more correctly if one said he wants to get on in life. Ambition is something so rare. We've got into the habit of calling someone ambitious if he wants to become a minister of state. Minister of state—what's that? A petty wholesaler's income and hardly enough power to be able to help one's own relatives, much less impose one's ideas, if one has any. I don't mean to say I wouldn't mind being a minister myself, it's certainly a better job than the one I've got—only it shouldn't be called ambition. It's something else. In the days when I was ambitious I worked out a very pretty little plan for conquering the whole earth and rearranging things as they ought to be; and when, in the end, everything became so good it almost began to be boring, then I was going to stuff my pockets with as much money as I could lay hands on and creep away, vanish in some cosmopolis and sit at a corner café and drink absinth and enjoy seeing how everything went to the devil as soon as I wasn't on the scene any more. . . . But, anyhow, I like Klas Recke. He's good-looking and he has an unusual talent for arranging things pleasantly for himself in this vale of woe.

Markel, yes! By and large he is what he has always been. Nowadays he's a correspondent for a big newspaper, writing articles in the mood indignant, articles that are intended to be read seriously and which sometimes really deserve to be. A bit unshaven and shaggy in the mornings, maybe, but always elegant by evening and with a good humour that lights up with the street lamps. Beside him, Birck sat with absent eyes, wearing a big raincoat in all this heat; he wrapped it round him with a frozen gesture.

Markel turned to me and asked me if I would care to join this select circle of dipsomaniacs. I thanked him, but replied that I was shortly going home. And such was my intention, although in reality I felt no longing for my solitary room, and sat on a long while more, listening to the music from the Strömparterren as it penetrated clear and loud through the dusky silence of the town and looking across to where the Palace mirrored its blind staring windows in the waters of The Stream—a stream which just then was no stream, but lay glassy as a forest pool. And I looked at a little blue star which stood shivering over Rosenbad. I listened, too, to the conversation at the neighbouring table. They were talking of women and love, the question being: what is the cardinal condition for a man to enjoy himself thoroughly with a woman?

The bald gentleman said: That she's sixteen, dark-haired, slim, and has hot blood.

MARKEL, with a dreamy expression: That she's fat and plump.

BIRCK: That she's fond of me.

July 2

No, things are beginning to become too horrible. Today, about ten in the morning, Mrs Gergorius stood in my room again. She looked pale and wretched, and her eyes were wide as they stared at me—What's the matter, I asked. What has happened—has something happened?

She answered in a low voice.

—Last night he raped me. As good as raped me.

I sat in my chair at the desk, my fingers playing with a pen and a piece of paper, as if about to write out a prescription. She sat in the corner of the sofa.—Poor child, I said, as if to myself. I couldn't find anything else to say.

She said:

—I'm made to be trampled on.

We fell silent a moment. Then she began to talk. He had woken her up in the middle of the night. Unable to sleep, he had begged and pleaded. Wept. Said his salvation was at stake. Didn't know what grievous sins he might not commit if she did not give in to his wishes.

It was her duty to do so; and duty came before health. God would help them. God would anyway give her back her health.

I sat dumbfounded.

—Is he a hypocrite, then? I asked, at length.

—I don't know. No, I don't think so. But he has got into the habit of using God for everything under the sun, as suits him best. They always do it, I know so many clergymen. I hate them. But he isn't a hypocrite; on the contrary, he has always thought it self-evident his religion is the right one, and so he tends to regard those who reject it as swindlers, wicked people who are intentionally telling lies in order to bring others to perdition.

She spoke calmly, but with a little tremble in her voice. In a way, what she said surprised me. Up to now I hadn't realised that this little feminine creature ever did any thinking, or that she was able so clearly, and as it were from the outside, to weigh up such a man as she was speaking of, even though she must surely feel a deadly hatred for him, a deep disgust. I felt that disgust, that hatred, in every tremulous word she uttered; and as she told her tale to the end, it infected me, too. She had wanted to get up, get dressed, go out into the streets all night, till morning came. But he held her fast. He was strong. Wouldn't let her go. . . .

I felt myself burn, my temples were beating in my head, inside me I heard a voice, so clear I was almost afraid I was thinking aloud, a voice whispering between its teeth: Beware, priest! I've promised this little woman, this feminine flower with the silken hair, over there, that I shall protect her against you. Beware, your life is in my hands. And before you want to go there I both can and will send you to paradise! You don't know me. My conscience bears not the least resemblance to yours. I am my own judge. I belong to a species of human being you do not even suspect exists!

Could she really be sitting there, listening to my thoughts? A little shiver ran through me as I suddenly heard her say:

—I could murder that man.

—My dear Mrs Gregorius, I said with a faint smile. Naturally that's only a manner of speaking. But it's one that shouldn't be used, even as such.

It had been on the tip of my tongue to say: least of all as such!

—But tell me, I went on in almost the same breath, and to change the subject. Tell me how it really came about that you married Mr Gregorius? Pressure from your parents; or perhaps a little infatuation at confirmation time?

She shuddered as if chilled.

—No, nothing like that, she said. It all happened in such a strange way, it was nothing you could guess at or understand of your own accord. Naturally, I was never in love with him, never in the least. Not even the usual girlish calf-love for the clergyman who confirmed me—nothing at all! But I'll try to explain. I'll tell you the whole story.

She settled deeper into the sofa. Hunched up like a little girl, and gazing beyond me and into abstraction, she began to speak:

—As a child and in my early youth I was so happy. When I think of that time it all seems like a fairy-story. Everyone liked me and I was fond of everyone. Then I came to that age . . . you know. But at first it made no difference. I was still perfectly happy, yes, happier than before—up to my twentieth year. A young girl, too, has her sensuality, as you understand; but in her earliest youth it's only a source of happiness to her. The blood sang in my ears, and I sang too—I was always singing as I went about my chores in the home, and when I walked down the street I used to hum under my breath. And I was always in love. I had grown up in a very religious home; but I didn't think it a terrible sin to be kissed. When I was in love with some young man and he kissed me, I just let it happen. I knew there was something else, too, which you had to look out for and which was a terrible sin, but it was all so dim and far-away to me, and I wasn't tempted. No, not at all. I didn't even understand that it could tempt anyone, I thought it was just something you had to submit to when you were married and wanted children, certainly nothing that could have any meaning in itself. But when I was twenty I fell deeply in love with a man.

He was good-looking and kind and sensitive—at least, so I thought then, and whenever I think of him I still believe it. Yes, he must be—later he married a girlhood friend of mine, and he has made her very happy. It was summer when we first met, out in the country. We kissed. One day he took me deep into the forest. There he tried to seduce me, and he came close to succeeding. Oh, if only he had succeeded, if only I hadn't run away—how different everything could have been now! Then I might have married him, perhaps— at least I shouldn't have married the man who is my husband today. Perhaps I would have had little children and a home, a real home; and should never have needed to become a faithless wife.—But I was wild with fear and shame. I squirmed out of his arms and ran away, ran for my life.

A terrible time followed. I didn't want to see him any more, dared not. He sent me flowers, wrote letter after letter, begging me to forgive him. But I thought he was a scoundrel. I left his letters unanswered and,

as for his flowers, I threw them out of the window.—
But I thought of him constantly. And now it was no
longer only kisses I thought about; now I knew what
temptation was. Although nothing had happened, I
felt as if some change had occurred in me. I imagined
others could see it written on me. No one can understand how I suffered. In the autumn, when we had
moved back into town, I was out walking on my own
one evening in the twilight. The wind whined round
the corners of the houses, and now and then a raindrop
fell. I entered the street where I knew he lived, and
walked past his house. Seeing a light burning in his
window, I stopped, and in the lamplight saw his head
bowed over a book. It attracted me like a magnet. I
thought how nice it would be to be in there with him.
I crept in through the doorway and was already halfway
up the stairs—but then I turned back.

If he had written to me in those days I should have
answered. But he had tired of writing without ever
getting any reply, and so we never met again—not for
many years. And by then, of course, everything was
quite different.

I've told you already, haven't I, that I was very
religiously brought up. Now I sank wholly into religion.
I began training to be a nurse, but had to give it up
because my health had begun to fail. So I came home
again, did odd jobs about the house as before, and
dreamed and had longings and prayed to God to free
me from my dreams and my longings. I felt things were
unbearable as they were, and that there must be a
change. Then one day I heard from Father that the
Rev. Gregorius had asked for my hand in marriage. I
was utterly astounded. He had never made me any
advances, never given me the least intimation. He was
an old friend of the family. Mother admired him. And

Father, I think, was a bit scared of him. I went to my room and cried. In some special way I had always felt there was something repulsive about him; I believe it must have been this which made me decide to say yes. No one forced me. No one argued me into it. But I believed it was God's will. Hadn't I always been taught to believe that God's will was always that which most contradicted our own? Hadn't I lain awake, only last evening, praying to God for freedom and peace? Now I believed He had heard my prayers—in His own way. I thought I saw His will shining clearly before my eyes. Beside that man, so I fancied, my longings would be extinguished and desire die away. In this way, I thought, God had arranged things for me. And I was sure he must be a good and a fine man, since he was a clergyman.

Well, it all turned out quite differently. He wasn't able to kill my dreams. He could only besmirch them. Instead, little by little, he killed my faith. This is the only thing I have to thank him for, because I certainly don't want it back again. Faith—when I think of it now, it seems merely queer. Everything one longed for, everything delightful to think about, was sin. A man's embraces were sin, if one longed for them and really wanted them; but if one found them ugly and repulsive, a scourge, a torment, something disgusting—then it was sin *not* to desire them! Tell me, Doctor Glas, isn't that queer?

She had grown hot from talking. I nodded to her over my glasses:

—Yes, it's queer.

—Or tell me, do you believe my love now is sin? It isn't only happiness. Perhaps, even more, it's anxiety. But do you think it's sin? If it is sin, then everything in me is sin, since I can't find anything in myself that is better or more valuable.—But perhaps you're surprised at me, sitting here and talking to you about all this. After all, I have someone else I can talk to. But when we meet our time is so short, and he talks to me so little—she blushed suddenly—so little about the things I think of most.

I sat quiet and silent with my head in my hand, observing her through half-closed eyes as she sat there in the corner of my sofa, rosy-hued under her rich yellow hair. The Maiden Silkencheek. I thought: if she had these feelings for me, there wouldn't be time for talk either. And I thought: When she next begins to speak I'll go over to her and close her mouth with a kiss. But now she sat silent. The door to my big waiting room was ajar, and I heard my housekeeper's footsteps in the corridor.

I broke the silence.

—But tell me, Mrs Gregorius, haven't you ever considered divorce? You're not tied to your husband by any economic necessity—your father left a fortune, you were his only child, and your mother's still alive, in good circumstances. Isn't that so?

—Ah, Doctor Glas, you don't know him. Divorce— a clergyman! He'd never agree to it, never! Whatever I did, whatever happened. He would sooner 'forgive' me seventy times over, rehabilitate me, everything imaginable. . . . He'd even be capable of holding prayers for me in church.—No, I'm made to be trampled on.

I got up:

—Well, my dear Mrs Gregorius, what do you want me to do now? I can't see any way out any more.

At a loss, she shook her head.

—I don't know. I don't know anything any more. But I think he's coming to see you today about his heart. He mentioned it yesterday. Couldn't you speak to him, just once more? Of course without letting him suspect I've been here today and spoken to you about this?

—Well—we'll see.

She left.

When she had gone, I took up a medical journal to distract my thoughts. But it was no use. I kept on seeing her before me, telling me her life-story and how it came about that she had got into such an impossible situation. Whose fault was it? Was it the fault of that man who had tried to seduce her in the forest, one summer's day? Alas, what is a man's business with a woman in this world of ours, if not to seduce her, whether in the forest or in the bridal bed, and then help and support her in all that follows? Whose fault was it, then— was it the clergyman's? After all he had only desired her, as thousands of men have desired thousands of women, desired her quite honourably into the bargain, as they call it in their queer jargon—and she, without, knowing or understanding anything, merely influenced by the strange confusion of ideas in which she had grown up, had consented. When she married that creature she was not awake, she did it in her sleep. And in dreams of course the oddest things occur, though they seem completely natural and ordinary—in dreams. But when one is awake and remembers what one has dreamt, one is astounded, and either laughs out loud or else shivers with fear. Now she has woken up! And her parents, who, after all, ought to have known what marriage is but gave their consent even so, and perhaps were even delighted and flattered—were they awake? And the clergyman himself: did he have the least sense of how unnatural, how grossly indecent his behaviour was?

Never have I had so strong a feeling that morality is

a merry-go-round, a spinning top. I knew this before, of course; but I had always imagined its phases must be centuries or aeons—now they seemed to me to be minutes or seconds. There was a flickering before my eyes. And inside me, my only guide in this witches' dance, I heard again a voice whisper between its teeth: Have a care, priest!

*　　　*　　　*

Quite correct. He came to my surgery hour. Inside me as I opened the door and saw him sitting out there in the waiting-room, I felt a sudden secret merriment. There was only one patient before him, an old woman who wanted her prescription renewed—then it was his turn. Spreading out the tails of his coat he sat down with ponderous dignity in the same corner of the sofa as his wife had sat hunched up in a few hours before.

As usual, he began by talking a lot of drivel. The communion question was what he now entertained me with. As for his heart trouble, that only came out in passing, in parenthesis, and I received the impression that he had really come to hear my opinion as a doctor on the question (at present being debated by all the newspapers by way of relief from the Great Lake Monster), as to whether Holy Communion constitutes a danger to people's health. I haven't followed this discussion, though now and then I've seen some article on the matter in a newspaper and half-read it. But I was far from being well-informed on the subject, and instead it was the clergyman who had to expound the situation to me. What is to be done to prevent infection at the communion table? That was the question. The vicar very much regretted it had ever been raised. But now it had been raised, and so it must be answered. Various solutions could be envisaged. Perhaps the simplest would be if each church acquired a number of small beakers which the verger could clean at the altar after every group of communicants—but this would be expensive, and perhaps it might even be impossible for poor country parishes to acquire a sufficient number of silver cups.

I remarked casually that in our time, when interest in religion is steadily on the increase and masses of silver cups are bought up for every bicycle race, it should not prove impossible to get hold of identical cups for religious purposes. For the rest, I do not remember a single word about silver appearing in the institution of Holy Communion; but this reflection I kept to myself.—Further, the Vicar went on, the possibility had been considered of every communicant bringing his own cup or glass. But how would it look if the rich brought along artistically embellished silver cups and the poor, maybe, a brandy glass?

For my part I thought it would look rather picturesque; but I held my peace and let him continue.— Then, he went on, there was a clergyman of the modern, free-thinking variety who had suggested that Our Saviour's blood could be swallowed in capsules.—At first I wondered if I had heard him aright. In capsules, like castor oil?—Yes, in capsules. Finally one of the Court Chaplains had constructed a communion cup of an entirely new sort, patented it and formed a limited company. The Vicar described the invention for me in detail. It seemed to be designed along more or less the same lines as a conjurer's glasses and bottles. Well, the Rev. Gregorius, for his part, is orthodox. He is nothing of a free-thinker. These innovations, one and all, fill him with profound misgivings. But so, too, do germs. So what's to be done?

As I heard him utter this word, a light dawned.

Instantly, I recognised the tone of voice. Once before I recalled hearing him speak of germs; and now it was at once clear to me he was suffering from the disease known as bacillophobia. In his eyes, evidently, germs lie mysteriously beyond the pale equally of religion and our system of conventions. This, of course, is because they are so new. His religion is old, almost nineteen hundred years old, and as for our system of social conventions, it dates at very least from the beginning of the nineteenth century, from German philosophy and the fall of Napoleon. But germs, assailing him in his old age, have taken him completely off his guard. According to his way of seeing things it has not been until this lattermost age that they have begun their nasty activities, certainly it has never occurred to him that, as far as we can judge, there must also have been masses of germs in the simple earthenware pot which passed round the Table at the Last Supper in Gethsemane.

Impossible to decide, whether he's more fool or fox.

I turned my back on him and let him talk, meanwhile arranging something in my instrument cupboard. Casually, I asked him to take off his coat and waistcoat; as for the communion question, without more ado I decided my vote should go to the capsule method.

—I admit, I said, at first glance this idea did seem a bit objectionable, even to me; though I certainly cannot boast any warm religiosity. But, on closer reflexion, all objections must be waived. Surely, the essence of the communion does not lie in the bread and wine, nor even in the church plate, but in faith. And true faith obviously cannot let itself be influenced by such outward things as silver cups and gelatine pills. . . .

With these last words I put my stethoscope to his chest, asked him to be quiet a moment, and listened. It was nothing remarkable I heard, in there. Only the slight irregularity of the heart movements which is so usual in an elderly man who is in the habit of eating more for dinner than he needs, and then rolling himself up for a snooze on the sofa. One day it can lead to a stroke. One can never be sure of course; and it is by no means inevitable. Not even a particularly threatening possibility.

But my mind was made up. This was going to be a serious consultation. I listened, much longer than necessary. Moved the tube. Tapped. Listened again. I noticed how it pained him, having to sit silent, passive, under all this—he's used to talking incessantly, in church, in company, in his home. He has indeed, a distinct talent for it. And this little talent, it must have been, which first attracted him to his calling. My examination frightened him a bit—probably he would have preferred to run on awhile about his communion pills, and then, with a sudden glance at his watch, make a dash for the door. But now I had him on my sofa. And I wasn't letting him slip away. Silently, I listened. And the longer I listened, the more troublesome his heart became.

—Is it serious? he asked, at length.

I did not answer immediately. Instead, I took a few paces across the floor. A plan was fermenting in my mind. In itself, it was quite a simple little plan. Even so, unpractised as I am in intrigue, I hesitated. And if I did so, it was also for the good reason that my whole plan was based on his stupidity and ignorance—but . . . was he stupid enough? Did I dare? Or was it too crude? Perhaps he saw through me?

I broke off my promenade. For a couple of seconds I threw him my very sharpest doctor's glance. The greyish white, podgy face lay in its sheepish pious folds.

But his eyes eluded me. His spectacles reflected only my window, its curtains, and my rubber plant. I decided to be bold. Sheep or fox—I thought—even a fox is much more stupid than a human being. With him there was decidedly no risk in playing the charlatan awhile—he liked charlatan tricks, so much was obvious: my pensive promenade to and fro across the floor and my long silence after his questions had already impressed him, softened him up.

—Queer, I mumbled at last, as if to myself.

And again I approached him with the stethoscope.

—Forgive me. But I must listen just a little while longer. I must be quite sure I'm not making a mistake.

—Well, I said, at length. To judge from what I hear today, that's not a strong heart you've got, Vicar. But somehow or other I can't think it's all that bad in the ordinary way of things. I fancy it has its special reasons for giving trouble today!

Hurriedly, not quite successfully, he tried to re-form his face into a question-mark. I saw at once his bad conscience had comprehended me. His lips worked as if about to speak, ask me, perhaps, what I meant. But, not managing it, he merely coughed. Certainly, he would have preferred to avoid any closer explanations —but I was not letting him escape me.

—Let us be honest with one another, Mr Gregorius, I began.

At this opening he jumped with fright.

—You have certainly not forgotten the conversation we had a couple of weeks ago, about your wife's health. It is not my intention to put any awkward questions, as to how you've kept the agreement then reached. I will merely say, Vicar, that had I known then how your heart was, I could have adduced even stronger reasons for the advice I then permitted myself to give you. For your wife, it's a question of her health, over a longer or shorter period. For you, it can easily be a question of your life.

He looked horrible as I spoke—a sort of colour came into his face, but nothing reddish, only green and mauve. I had to turn away, he was so dreadfully ugly to look at. I went over to the open window to get a breath of fresh air; but it was almost more oppressive outdoors than in.

I went on:

—My prescription is clear and simple: it reads 'separate bedrooms'. I remember you don't like it, but that can't be helped. For it isn't only ultimate satisfaction which, in this case, involves a grave risk; it's also important to avoid everything which can whet or excite your desires.—Yes, yes, I know what you're going to say; that you're an old man, and a clergyman to boot; but after all, I am a doctor, and I've the right to speak openly to a patient. And I don't think I'm exceeding the bounds of what is reasonable if I point out that the constant propinquity of a young woman, particularly at nights, must have much the same effect on a clergyman as on any other mortal man. I've studied at Uppsala. I knew many theologians there. And I did not exactly gain the impression that theological studies were more efficient than others as a fire insurance for young bodies against this sort of outbreak. As for age—well, how old are you, sir?—fifty-seven; it's a critical age. At your age desire is much the same as it ever was,—but satisfaction brings in its revenges. Well, it's true there are many ways of looking at life, and various ways of evaluating it; and if it was an old rake I was speaking to I should naturally be prepared to hear from him an answer logical enough, seen from his point of view: To the devil with all that! There's no sense in forsaking the thing which gives life its value, merely in order to retain life itself. But of course I know such a way of reasoning is wholly foreign to your way of thinking, Vicar. My duty as a doctor in this case is to warn and enlighten—this is all I can do, and I am certain, now you know how serious it is, nothing more will prove needful. I find it hard to believe it would be to your taste to drop dead like the late-lamented King Frederick I or, more recently, M. Félix Faure. . . .

I avoided looking at him as I spoke. But when I had made an end, I saw he was sitting there with his hand over his eyes, and that his lips were moving. And I guessed, rather than heard: Our Father, which art in Heaven, hallowed be Thy name . . . lead us not into temptation, but deliver us from evil. . . .

I sat down at my desk, adding as I handed him the prescription:

—And staying in town all through this hot summer isn't good for you, either. A visit to the waters would do you a world of good. Porla; or Ronneby. But in that case, of course, you must go alone.

July 5

Summer Sunday. Everything stiflingly close and dusty, and only the poorer sort of people stirring abroad. And the poor, alas, are not congenial.

About four I went and sat down on board a little steamer to have dinner at Djurgårdsbrunn. My housekeeper had gone to a funeral. Afterwards she was to drink coffee out in the open air. The dead person was no relative or friend of hers, but for that class of woman a funeral is always a great pleasure and I hadn't the heart to refuse my permission. This meant that I, too, must dine out. As a matter of fact, acquaintances had invited me to their villa in the archipelago; but I did not feel like it. I have no particular liking for acquaintances or villas in the archipelago. Least of all for the archipelago. A mincemeat landscape, all chopped up. Little islands, little waterways, little rocky knolls and wretched little trees. A pale and poverty-stricken landscape, cold colours, mostly grey and blue, and yet not poor enough to have the grandeur of true desolation. When I hear people praise the archipelago's natural beauties I always suspect them of having quite other things in mind and on closer examination this suspicion is always confirmed. One person thinks of the fresh air and fine bathing, another of his sailing boat, a third of the perch-fishing, yet for them all this falls under the rubric of natural beauty. The other day I was talking to a young girl who was in love with the archipelago but, as our conversation proceeded, it transpired that in point of fact she was thinking of sunsets; possibly also of a student. She forgot that the sun sets everywhere and that students are mobile. I do not believe I am wholly insensitive to natural beauty, but for that I must go further afield, to Lake Vättern or Skåne, or else to the sea. But I rarely have time, and within a radius of twenty or thirty miles of Stockholm I have never seen a landscape to compare with Stockholm itself —with Djurgården or Haga or the pavement overlooking the Stream, outside The Grand. This is why I mostly stay in town, summer and winter. I do this the more willingly, having the solitary person's constant desire to see people around me—*nota bene*, people I do not know and so do not have to speak to.

So I arrived at Djurgårdsbrunn and found a table by the glass wall in the long pavilion. The waiter hurried forward with the menu and discreetly spread a clean white napkin over the remains of gravy and Batty's mustard left by an earlier party. The next moment, handing me the wine list, he disclosed by his hasty 'Chablis'? a memory containing, it may be, depths of knowledge immeasurable as many a professor's. No regular winebibber, it is true that when dining out I never drink any other wine but Chablis. And he was an old hand who knew his man. His first youthful frenzies he had stilled balancing punch trays at Berns, afterwards with the seriousness of riper years fulfilling the more involved duties of dining-room waiter at Rydberg and Hamburger Börs. Who knows what transient rejection at destiny's hands was now responsible for him —hair thinning and evening dress a trifle frayed— labouring at his calling in this somewhat humbler place? The years had lent him an air of belonging wherever there is a smell of food and bottles to be uncorked. I was pleased to see him, and we exchanged a glance of secret understanding.

I looked round at the clientèle. At the next table sat the pleasant young man I usually buy my cigars from. He was treating his girl friend, a tasty little shop assistant with sharp mousey eyes. A little further away sat an actor with his wife and children, wiping his mouth with sacerdotal gravity. And, in a corner, a solitary old eccentric whom I must have seen in the streets and cafés these twenty years, sharing his dinner with his dog. The dog, too, was old and his fur had gone a little grey.

The Chablis had come and I was sitting enjoying the play of sunbeams in the light wine in my glass when, quite close at hand, I heard a woman's voice that seemed familiar. I looked up. A family had just come in. Husband. Wife. And a little four- or five-year-old boy, a very pretty lad, but stupidly—indeed ridiculously—dressed up in a pale blue velvet blouse and lace collar. It was the wife who did the talking and it was her voice which had sounded so familiar.—We'll sit over there,—no, not there,—that's in the sun—no, there we won't have any view—where's the head waiter?

All at once I recognised her. It was the same young woman who had once writhed weeping on the floor of my room, begging and pleading with me to help her—to free her of the child she was expecting. Afterwards she had got married to the oaf she had so desired, and had her child—a bit too quickly, but that makes no odds, now. So here we have the *corpus delictii*; in velvet blouse and lace collar. Well, my little lady, and what do you say now—wasn't I right? The scandal passed over; but your little boy is left to you, and you have the pleasure of him. . . .

Yet, I wonder whether it really is that child? No, it can't be. The lad is four, at most five, and it's at least seven or eight years since that old story. It was at the very beginning of my practice. What can have happened to the first child? Perhaps it has come to grief in some way. Well, that's of no importance—they seem to have repaired the damage afterwards.

Anyway I don't much care for this family. On closer inspection I see the wife is young and still quite beautiful, but she has put on a good deal of weight and her complexion is almost too blooming. I suspect her of passing her mornings sitting in cake-shops, drinking stout to her pastries and gossiping with women friends. And the master of the household is a counter-jumper Don Juan. From his appearance and manner, I should judge him faithless as a cock. Furthermore, they both have that habit of scolding the waiter in advance for the negligence they expect of him: a habit which makes me feel sick. In a word, scum.

I washed down my mixed impressions with a deep draught of the light acidulous wine, and gazed out through the great wide sliding windows. Out there, rich and quiet, the landscape lay warm in the evening sun. The canal mirrored the greenery on its banks and the blue of the sky. Quietly, lightly, a couple of canoes, paddled by men in striped blue sweaters, slid in under the bridge and vanished, bicyclists spun over the bridge and scattered over the roads, and in the grass beneath the big trees people were sitting in groups, enjoying the shade and the beautiful day. While over my table fluttered two yellow butterflies.

And while I sat like that, letting my gaze sink into the summer greenery out there, my thoughts idled into a fantasy with which I divert myself at times. I have a little money saved up, ten thousand crowns or a little more, in good securities. In five or six years or so I shall perhaps have saved enough to be able to build myself a house out in the country. But where shall I build it? It has to be by the sea. It must be on an open coast, without islands or skerries. I want an open horizon, and I want to *hear* the sea. And I want the sea to lie to westward. The sun must set in it.

But there is one more thing, as important as the sea; I want to have a wealth of greenery and great sighing trees. No pines or spruces. Well, pines are acceptable, providing they are tall and straight and strong and have succeeded in becoming what they are intended to be; but the jagged contour of a spruce forest against the sky causes me an inexplicable sadness. Furthermore, in the country as in the town, it sometimes rains and a spruce forest in rainy weather makes me feel ill and depressed. No, it must be an Arcadian meadow, sloping gently towards the beach, with clumps of big leafy umbrageous trees, a vaulting of greenery, above my head.

But, alas, the coastal scenery is not like that; it is

mean and raw. The sea-breezes make the trees knotty, small, dwarfish. I shall never set eyes on the coast where I wish to build and live.

And then, building a house; this, too, is an endless business. It takes a couple of years before it's ready. Probably, during that time, you go and die. Then it takes two or three more years before it's in order, and then there's a wait of about another fifty years or so before a house becomes really agreeable to live in.

A wife, too, should really be part of the scheme. But that isn't always plain sailing, either. I find it so difficult to stomach the idea of someone looking at me while I'm asleep. A child's sleep is beautiful, a young woman's too; but hardly a man's. It's said that a hero's slumber by his camp-fire, his head pillowed on his knapsack, is lovely to behold; and this is possible, for he is so weary and sleeps so sound. But what can my face look like when my thoughts are in a coma? I should scarcely enjoy seeing it myself, if I could—still less should anybody else.

No. The dream of happiness does not exist that does not bite its own tail.

I often wonder, too, what character I should prefer for myself had I never read a book or seen a work of art. In that event perhaps it would not even occur to me to choose—perhaps the archipelago, with its rocks, would do for me. All my thoughts and dreams about Nature are most probably based on impressions drawn from poetry and art. From art I have acquired my longing to wander at ease in the ancient Florentine's flowery meadows and nod on Homer's seas and bend the knee in Böcklin's sacred grove. Alas, what would my own poor eyes see of this world, left to themselves without all these hundreds and thousands of teachers and friends among those who have sung and thought and

seen on behalf of all the rest of us? Often in my youth
I have thought: To have been there! To have had the
chance! To be allowed to give, for once, and not always
receive. It's so dreary, always moving on alone, with a
soul barren of fruit, at one's wits' end to know what to
do to feel that one is something, means something, or
to have a little respect for oneself. Probably it's a most
happy state of affairs that most people are so undemanding in this respect. I have not been undemanding,
and long it has pained me; though I believe the worst
is over now.

I could hardly have become a poet—I see nothing
which others haven't seen already and given form to.
Of course I know a few authors and artists; queer
creatures, in my view. There's nothing they have a will
to; or, if there is, then they do the opposite. They are
just ears and eyes and hands. Yet I envy them. Not that
I would exchange my will for their visions, but I should
very much like to have their eyes and ears into the
bargain. Sometimes when I see one of them sitting
silent, absent-minded, staring into emptiness, I think
to myself: perhaps at this very moment he sees something no one has seen before and which he will shortly
oblige a thousand others to see, myself among them.
What the youngest among them produce I certainly do
not understand—as yet—but I also know and foresee
that, once they are recognised and known, I, too, will
understand and admire them. It is the same as with
new modern clothes, furniture, everything else; only
those who have become rigid, dried up, who long ago
are finished and done with, can resist them. And the
poets themselves, are they really the legislators of the
age? God knows, But they hardly look like it to me.
Rather I should say they are the instruments the age
plays upon, aeolian harps the wind sings in. And what

am I? Not even that. I have no eyes of my own. I can hardly see the drinkers and the radishes on the table, over there, with my own eyes; I see them with Strindberg's and think of a supper he ate in his youth at Stallmästaregården. And when the canoeists flew past on the canal, just now, in their striped vests, it seemed to me for a moment as if the shade of Maupassant fled on before them

And now, as I sit at my open window, writing this by a flickering candle—I detest touching oil-lamps and my housekeeper is sleeping too soundly after her funeral coffee and cakes for me to have the heart to wake her—now, as the candleflame flutters in the draught and my shadow shivers and flutters like the flame on the wallpaper, as if trying to come to life— now I think of Hans Andersen and his tale of the shadow. And it seems to me I am the shadow who wished to become a man.

July 6, in the morning

I must make a note of the dream I had last night.

I stood at the Rev. Gregorius's bedside; he was ill. The upper part of his body was bared and I was listening to his heart. The bed stood in his study; a harmonium stood in one corner and someone was playing on it. No hymn tune, hardly a melody. A door was open; it worried me, but I could not bring myself to have it closed.

—Is it serious? asked the clergyman.

—No, I replied, it's not serious; but it's dangerous.

I meant that what I was thinking of was dangerous to myself. And in my dream I thought I had expressed myself with profundity and elegance.

—But for safety's sake, I added, we may as well send to the chemist's for some communion pills.

—Must I be operated on? asked the clergyman.
I nodded.

—It looks like it. Your heart is no use at all, it's too old. We'll have to take it out. But don't worry, it's a perfectly safe operation, it can be done with an ordinary paper-knife.

This seemed to me quite a simple scientific truth, and it so happened I had a paper-knife in my hand.

—We'll just lay this handkerchief over your face.

The clergyman groaned aloud under the handkerchief. But instead of operating I swiftly pressed a button in the wall.

I took away the handkerchief. He was dead. I felt his hand; it was stone cold. I looked at my watch.

—He's been dead for at least two hours, I said to myself.

Mrs Gregorius got up from the organ, where she had been sitting and playing and came up to me. Her look seemed worried and sorrowful and she handed me a posy of dark flowers. It was only then I saw she was smiling ambiguously, and that she was naked.

I held out my arms to her and wanted to draw her to me, but she eluded me, and instantly Klas Recke was standing in the open doorway.

—Doctor Glas, he said, in my capacity of temporary departmental chief I declare you under arrest!

—It's too late now, I told him. Don't you see anything?

I pointed to the window. A red flash burst in through both the windows of the room; suddenly it was broad daylight, and a woman's voice that seemed to come from another room whined and whimpered: The world's on fire, the world's on fire!

And I woke up.

The morning sun was shining straight into the

room. Last night when I came home I'd forgotten to draw down the blind.

Odd. These last days I haven't been thinking about the ugly parson and his beautiful wife at all. Haven't *wanted* to think about them.

And Gregorious has anyway gone to Porla.

*   *   *

I do not write down all my thoughts here.

I seldom write down a thought the first time it comes to me. I wait and see if it recurs.

July 7

It's raining, and I'm sitting thinking about unpleasant things.

Why did I say 'no' to Hans Fahlén that time last autumn, when he came and asked to borrow fifty crowns? True, I hardly knew him. But next week he cut his throat.

And why didn't I learn Greek when I was at school? It makes me feel almost ill with annoyance. After all, I studied it for four years. Was it perhaps because my father had forced me to study it instead of English that I persevered in learning nothing? How can one be so brutishly stupid! Didn't I learn everything else, including that nonsense called logic. Yet I studied Greek for four years, but know no Greek.

And it can't possibly have been my teacher's fault, for he afterwards became a Minister of State.

I should like to dig out my school books again and see whether I can learn anything now; perhaps it is not too late.

*   *   *

JULY 9

I wonder what it feels like to have a crime on one's conscience.

*   *   *

I wonder whether Christina won't soon have dinner ready.

*   *   *

The wind shakes the trees in the churchyard, and the rain chatters in the roof gutters. A poor devil with a bottle in his pocket has sought shelter under the church roof, in a corner of a buttress. He stands propped against the red church wall, his gaze straying blue and pious among the driving clouds. The rain drips from the two lean trees by Bellman's grave. Across this corner of the churchyard, a little to one side, stands a house of ill fame; a girl in her petticoat pads over to a window and draws down the blind.

But down among the graves the vicar of the parish picks his cautious way through the mud in galoshes, stalking under his umbrella, and now he creeps in through the little door into the vestry.

*   *   *

By the way, why do the clergy always go into church by a back door?

July 9

It's still raining. Days like these are kin with all the secret poison in my soul.

Just now, on my way home from visiting patients, I exchanged greetings at a street corner with a man I do not like to meet. He insulted me once—deeply, politely, and in such circumstances that I see no chance of repaying him.

Such things I do not like. They touch my health.

*   *   *

I sit at my desk, opening one drawer after another and looking at old papers and things. A little yellowed newspaper clipping falls into my hands.

Is there a life after this? by H. Cremer theol. dr. Price: 50 öre.

John Bunyan's Revelations A survey of the life to come, Heaven's splendour and the horrors of Hell. Price: 75 öre.

 MAN'S OWN STRENGTH

The right way to distinction and riches by S. Smiles, Price: 3.50 eleg. bnd. in cl. w. glt l. 4.25

Why have I hidden this old advertisement? I remember cutting it out when I was fourteen, the year my father's fortune went up in smoke. Saving up my little pocket money I bought Mr Smiles' book, albeit without gold lettering. As soon as I had read it I sold it to a secondhand bookseller; it was too exaggeratedly stupid.

But I still have the advertisement. It is also more valuable.

And here is an old photograph: the country place we owned for a few years. Mariebo, it was called, after my mother.

The photograph is yellowed and faded, and a mist seems to hang over the white house and the spruce forest behind it. Yes, that is just how it looked there, on grey and rainy days.

Somehow I never really enjoyed myself there. Father beat me so during the summers. They say I was a fractious child at such times as I did not have school and lessons.

Once he beat me unjustly. This is almost one of my happiest childhood memories. Naturally, it hurt my skin; but it did my soul good. When I went down to the lake afterwards it was blowing half a gale and the foam was whipped up into my face. I'm not sure I have ever felt myself so deliciously flooded with noble feelings as I was then. I forgave my father; he was so quick-tempered; and he was also very much worried about his business.

It was harder to forgive him all those times when he beat me justly; I'm not sure I've forgiven him, even now. Like that time when, in spite of strictest prohibitions, I'd bitten my nails again. How he hit me! And for hours afterwards I wandered about in pouring rain in that wretched spruce forest, and cried and swore.

There was never really anything peaceful about my father. He was rarely cheerful, and when he wasn't, could not abide the cheerfulness of others. But he liked parties; he was of the company of melancholy wastrels. He was rich, and died poor. To this day I do not know whether he was completely honest; after all, he was involved in such big transactions. How I pondered, as a child, some words I once heard him let fall in jest to one of his business acquaintances: "Well, my dear Joseph, it isn't so easy to be honest when one is earning such big money as we are. . . ." But he was strict and hard and had perfectly clear and definite ideas about duty, where others were concerned. For oneself one can always find circumstances that alter cases.

But the worst thing was that I always felt for him such a strong physical revulsion. How it tormented me when, as a little boy, I had to bathe with him and he wanted to teach me to swim. I slithered like an eel out of his hands, again and again thought I was going to drown and was almost as scared of death as I was of coming into contact with his naked body. Certainly he cannot have suspected how acutely this purely physical revulsion increased my pain when he beat me. And much later on, travelling in his company or for some other chance reason, it was a torment whenever I had to sleep in the same room with him.

Yet I was fond of him, even so. Perhaps mostly because he was so proud of my brains. And also because he was always so well-dressed. For a while I hated him. too, because he was unkind to my mother. But then she took ill and died. And then I noticed he mourned her more than I could, with my fifteen years, and so of course I couldn't hate him any longer.

Now they are both gone. And gone are they all—all those who walked and stood among the furniture in my childhood's home. Well, not all, but all those I cared for. My brother Ernst, who was so strong and so stupid and so kind, my help and protector in all the adventurous happenings of a schoolboy's life—gone. He went away to Australia, and no one knows whether he's alive or dead. And my beautiful cousin, Alice, who used to stand so pale and upright by the piano and sing with sleepwalker's eyes and in a voice that shimmered and burned, sang so that I was shaken with shivering in a corner of the great glassed-in verandah, sang as I shall never hear anyone else sing again. What became of her? Married to poverty, with a smalltown schoolteacher, already old and ill and worn-out. I fell into a sudden convulsion of weeping when I met her last Christmas in her mother's home, and she was affected, and we both wept. . . . And her sister Anna with the hot cheeks she who had the same fever in the dance as her sister had in song, she ran away from her scoundrelly husband, with another scoundrel, and was abandoned. Now, so they say, she lives off her body in Chicago.

And their father, the kind good-looking, witty Uncle
Ulrik, whom they always said I resembled, although I
resembled him in an ugly way, he was swept away in
the same crash that overthrew my father, dying, like
him, in poverty. .... What plague was it that tore them
all away, within a few short years, into the grave or a
shadowy life of misery, all, all, even most of those
friends who thronged our rooms in festal days gone by.

God knows what it was. But they are all gone.

And Mariebo; if I'm not mistaken, it's called Sofie-
lund, now.

July 10

At my writing-desk.

It occurs to me to press the spring which opens the
little secret drawer. Of course I know what lies there:
just a little round box with some pills in it. I don't want
to have them lying about in my medicine cupboard,
some confusion might arise one day, and that wouldn't
be a good thing. I made them up myself, a number of
years ago, and they contain a little potassium cyanide.
At the particular moment when I made them up I was
not thinking of taking my own life. But I was of the
opinion that a wise man should always be ready.

If you take a little potassium cyanide in a glass of
wine or suchlike, death follows instantly. The glass
slips from your hand and falls to the floor; it is clear to
one and all there has been a suicide. That is not always
desirable. If, on the other hand, you take one of my
pills and then drink a glass of water, a minute or two
will elapse before the pill has time to dissolve and take
effect. You have time to put the glass back quietly on
the tray, sit down in a comfortable chair and unfold
your *Aftonbladet.* Suddenly, you collapse. The doctor
reports a stroke. Naturally, if there is an autopsy, the

poison will be detected. But where there are no suspicious or particularly interesting circumstances from the medical point of view there is no obduction. And no such circumstances can be said to exist if someone has a stroke while reading *Aftonbladet* over his after-dinner cigar.

Therefore I am consoled to know that these flour-coated balls, resembling smallshot, are lying there, awaiting a day they may be needed. Within them slumbers a force, evil and hateful in itself, mankind's and all living things' enemy from the beginning. Only to be released when it becomes the one passionately desired liberator from a worse.

What was I most thinking of, when I made up these little black pills for myself? Suicide from unhappy love —that's something I've never been able to conceive. From poverty, rather. Of all so-called outward calamities poverty certainly takes the deepest inward toll. But it appears not to threaten me. Personally I regard myself as among the better-off, and sociologists would place me among the wealthy. What I was thinking of was illness. I have seen so much . . . cancer, blindness, paralysis. How many unfortunates have I not seen to whom I would not have felt the least compunction in administering one of these pills, if, in me as in other decent people, self-interest and respect for the law had not spoken louder than mercy. Instead, how much useless, hopelessly ruined human wreckage have I not helped to preserve in the course of my duties—not even blushing to take payment. But such is the custom; and in matters that do not affect us deeply or personally it is perhaps right we should. And why should I make a martyr of myself for a view which sooner or later must become the view of all civilised people, but which today is still criminal?

The day will come, must come, when the right to die is recognised as far more important and inalienable a human right than the right to drop a voting ticket into a ballot box. And when that time is ripe, every incurably sick person—and every 'criminal' also—shall have the right to the doctor's help, if he wishes to be set free.

There was something beautiful, grand about that cup of poison the Athenians, once believing his life was dangerous to the State, allowed the doctor to administer to Socrates. Our time, if it were to judge him in the same light, would have dragged him up on to a mean scaffold and slaughtered him with an axe.

*   *   *

Good-night, evil power. Sleep well in your little round box. Sleep till I need you. For me you shall have no untimely awakening. Today it's raining, but perhaps tomorrow the sun will shine. And not until that day dawns when even the sunshine seems pest-ridden and diseased shall I wake you, in order myself to sleep.

July 11

At my writing-desk, one grey rainy day.

In one of the little drawers I have just found a piece of paper on which some words were written in my own handwriting, as it looked some years ago—for everyone's handwriting changes ceaselessly, the tiniest little bit every year, unnoticed perhaps to oneself but as inevitably and surely as one's face, stance, movements, soul.

The words were: "Nothing so reduces and drags down a human being as the consciousness of not being loved."

When did I write that? Is it some reflection of my own, or a quotation I jotted down?

Don't remember.

* * *

I can understand the ambitious. I only have to sit in a corner of the Opera and hear the coronation march in *The Prophet* to feel a hot, if transient, longing to rule over humanity and have myself crowned in an old cathedral.

But it must be during my lifetime; the rest, for all I care, may be silence. Never have I understood those who go chasing after an immortal name. Humanity's memory is unjust and has its lapses, and we have forgotten our oldest and greatest benefactor. Who invented the cart? Pascal invented the wheelbarrow and Fulton the locomotive, but who invented the wheeled vehicle? No one knows. In return, history has preserved the name of King Xerxes' personal coachman: Patiramfes, son of Otanes. He drove the carriage of the great king. As for that blockhead who set fire to the Temple of Diana of Ephesus so that people should not forget his name, he certainly succeeded in his enterprise. You can look him up in Brockhaus.

* * *

We want to be loved; failing that, admired; failing that, feared; failing that, hated and despised. At all costs we want to stir up some sort of feeling in others. Our soul abhors a vacuum. At all costs it longs for contact.

July 13

I have grey days and black moments. I am not happy. Even so, I know no one with whom I would change

70

places; my heart shrinks at the thought of being this or that person among my acquaintance. No, I don't want to be any one else.

In early youth I suffered much from not having good looks and, in my burning desire for good looks, thought myself a monster of ugliness. Now, of course, I know I look very much like everyone else. Not exactly a source of rejoicing, this, either.

I am not particularly fond of myself, neither shell nor entrails. But I don't want to be anyone else.

July 14

Blessed sun, who hast the strength to seek us out, even down to the graves under the trees. . . .

Well, that was just now; now it's dark. I've come home from my evening walk. The town lay stretched out as if in a bath of roses, and over the southern heights hung a light rosy mist.

Awhile I sat alone at a table on the pavement outside The Grand and drank a little lemon cordial; just then Miss Martens came walking by. I got up and saluted her, and to my surprise she stopped, held out her hand and said a few words before going on her way, something about her mother's illness and the lovely evening. While she was speaking she blushed slightly, as if what she was doing was unusual and open to misinterpretation.

I at least did not misinterpret her. Many times I have noticed how soft and friendly, unaffected by all formality, her way is with almost everyone; and this has always pleased me.

But even so—how radiant she was! Is she in love with someone?

Her family was one of the many who suffered from my father's crash. Of recent years the old colonel's wife has been in bad health and she often uses my services. I have never wanted to accept any fee, and of course they understand why.

She rides, too; I have seen her several times recently during my morning rides, in fact as recently as yesterday. With a merry 'Good morning' she rode past me at top speed, then in the distance I saw her slow down at a curve in the road, and falling to a walk, ride on a long way with slackened reins, as if in a dream. . . . But I . . . I kept to my steady pace. In this way we rode past one another several times within a short space of time.

*   *   *

She isn't exactly beautiful, but there's something about her in some peculiar way close to what for many years, and up to quite recently, was my dream of woman. Such things can't be explained. Once, after a great deal of trouble—it must be two or three years ago now—I managed to get myself invited to the home of a family I knew she was friendly with, merely in order to meet her. And, indeed, she did turn up; but on that occasion she scarcely noticed me and we didn't exchange many words.

And now: I recognise her well enough. She is the same as she was then. It is myself I don't recognise.

July 17

No, sometimes life shows a face altogether too vile. Only a moment ago I came home from a night call. I was woken by the telephone ringing, took a name and address—it was quite close by—and a hint of what the trouble was: a child had suddenly fallen seriously ill, probably with the croup, at the home of so-and-so, a wholesaler. A cloud of drunken nightbirds and whores swarming about my coat-tails, I hurried through the streets. It was the fourth floor of a house in a side-street. The name I'd just heard on the telephone, and which I now saw on the front door, seemed familiar; although I could not place it. The wife received me in dressing-gown and petticoat,—it was the lady from Djurgårds-brunn, the same I remembered from that time years ago. So, I thought, it's the pretty little boy! I was shown through a narrow dining-room and an idiotic hallway, illuminated, just then, by a greasy kitchen lamp placed in the corner of a whatnot; and so into a bedroom. Evidently the master wasn't at home. "It's our eldest boy who is ill," the wife explained. She led me over to a little bed. In it lay, not the pretty little lad, but another, a monster. Enormous ape-like cheek-bones, a flattened cranium, little evil stupid eyes. It was obvious at first glance: an idiot.

So—this was her first-born! It was him she was carrying under her heart, that time. This was the seed she begged me on her knees to free her from; and I answered with duty. Life, I don't understand you!

And now death at last wished to take pity on him and on them, take him away from the life he should never have entered. But it's not to be. There is nothing they long for so much as to be quit of him. Yet their cowardly hearts impel them, even so, to send for me, the doctor, to drive away kind merciful death and keep this monster alive. And I, no less a coward, do 'my duty'—do it now, as I did then.

All these thoughts, of course, did not immediately pass through my head as I stood there, wide awake in that strange room, beside a sickbed. I merely followed my calling, thought nothing—stayed as long as was necessary, did what had to be done; and left. In the hall I met the husband and father, who had just come home, somewhat under the influence.

And the ape-boy is going to live—perhaps for many years yet. The loathsome brutish face with its evil stupid eyes pursues me, even into my room. I sit reading in them the whole story.

He has been given those very eyes the world looked at his mother with, when she was big with him. And with those same eyes the world fooled her into looking at what she had done.

And now, here's the fruit—a lovely fruit!

The brutal father who hit her, the mother whose head was full of what friends and relatives would say, the servants who looked askance at her, giggling and rejoicing in their hearts at this confirmation that their 'betters' are no better than their inferiors, aunts and uncles who became stiff with idiotic indignation and half-witted morality, the clergyman who made short work of his sermon at the humiliating wedding, a little embarrassed, perhaps rightly, at having to exhort the contracting parties on our Lord's behalf to do what so blatantly was already done—all, all contributed their mite, all had their little part in what ensued. Not even the doctor was missing—the doctor, that was me.

Couldn't I have helped her that time when, in her hour of utmost need and despair, she went down on her bended knees in this room? Instead, I replied with duty, in which I did not believe.

But neither could I know, or guess. . . .

Her case, at least, was one of those where I was sure of myself. Even if I did not believe in 'duty'—did not believe it to be the supremely binding law it gives itself out as being—yet it was perfectly clear to me that in this case the right, the prudent thing to do was what others call their duty. And I did not hesitate to do it.

Life, I don't understand you.

*   *   *

JULY 24

*   *   *

Every idiot at the Eugenia Home costs more in annual upkeep than a healthy young labourer earns in annual income.

July 24

The African heat has come back. All the afternoon it lies motionless over the town like a cloud of golden smoke. Not until dusk does it get cooler, bringing relief.

Almost every evening I sit for a while on the pavement outside The Grand, sipping light lemonade through a straw. I'm fond of the hour when the lamps begin to gleam in the curves along the quayside. It's the best hour of my day. Usually I sit there alone; but yesterday I sat with Birck and Markel.

—I praise God, said Markel, that they've begun to light the street lamps again. I don't know myself in the darkness of these lampless summer nights we've been wandering about in so long. Although I know this arrangement has been made exclusively for reasons of economy, a perfectly respectable motive, that is, I cannot help thinking it has, even so, a certain vulgar flavour of being arranged to suit the tastes of tourists. 'Land of the Midnight Sun'—to the devil!

—Yes, Birck agreed, they could at least content themselves with putting out the lights for two or three nights around midsummer, when it really is almost daylight. Out in the country these twilit summer nights of ours are quite magical, but here they don't belong at all. Street lights are a proper ingredient of a town. I've never felt the happiness and pride of being a townsman

75

so keenly as in my childhood when I came into town of
an autumn evening and saw the lamps alight round the
quays. Now, I thought to myself, now those poor
wretches out there in the country have got to stay
indoors if they don't want to stump about in darkness
and filth.

—Though it's true, he added, in the country there's
quite another sort of starry sky from what we have here.
Here, in competition with the gas-lamps, the stars
succumb. And that's a pity.

—The stars, said Markel, simply aren't up to lighting our footsteps as we wander about in the night. It's
sad to see how they've lost all practical importance.
Once they regulated our whole life; and to open an
ordinary penny-halfpenny almanack one would think
they still did. It would be difficult to find a more striking
instance of the toughness of tradition than the fact that
the most popular almanacks are full of detailed infor-
mation on matters which no living person any longer
cares a fig for. All these astronomical signs which the
poorest peasant had some idea of two hundred years
ago and studied diligently, believing his whole well-
being depended on them,—today they're unknown,
incomprehensible, to most educated people. If the
Academy of Science had any sense of humour it could
amuse itself by shuffling the Crab, the Lion and the
Virgin in its almanack, like lottery tickets in a hat, and
the public wouldn't be any the wiser. The starry sky
today has sunk to a purely decorative rôle.

He sipped his whisky, and went on:

—No, the stars can't congratulate themselves on
enjoying at all the same popularity they once had. As
long as one's fate was believed to hang on them, they
were feared, but also loved and worshipped. And as
children, of course, we all liked them. We imagined

they were pretty little lights God lit up in the evening
to amuse us. We thought it was us they were winking
at. But now we know rather more about them they're
only a constant, painful, insulting reminder of our own
insignificance. One evening, maybe, one takes a stroll
down Drottninggatan. One thinks thoughts, grandiose,
yes, even epoch-making thoughts; thoughts no human
being, one feels, has ever had the strength or courage
to think in this world before. Admittedly, somewhere
deep down in our unconscious, lurks the experience of
many years, whispering that, without a shadow of
doubt, tomorrow morning we shall either have forgotten
these same thoughts or else have no eye for their
grandiosity, their epoch-making qualities. It's all one.
As long as our thought-orgy lasts, nothing takes away
an iota from our happiness. But one only has to look up
by chance and see some tiny star sitting motionless
between a couple of tin chimneys, shining and winking,
to realise that one may as well forget them at once.
Or else you go walking along, looking down into the
gutter, wondering whether you're really right to drink
yourself to death, or whether, perhaps, there isn't some
better way of passing the time. Suddenly—and this
really happened to me the other night—one stops, and
gazes at a little sparkling point, down there in the
gutter. A moment of reflection—and one realises it's a
star that's mirrored there. To be precise it was Deneb,
in the Swan. And at once it becomes obvious how
absurdly unimportant the whole question is.

—Well, I permitted myself to remark, you can really
call that looking at drunkenness from the angle of
eternity. But it's hardly natural to us, while sober; and
the method is hardly suited, anyway, to daily use. If the
star Deneb were to hit on the idea of looking at itself
sub specie asternitatis it would realise perhaps how al-

together insignificant it is, and not take the trouble to shine any more. As things are, however, there it sits, for some while now, faithful at its post, and shines very prettily, doubtless mirroring itself not only in the oceans of planets unknown, whose sun it is, but even, now and then, in a gutter on our dark little earth. Follow its example, my dear chap! That's to say: generally speaking, and by and large—not only where the gutter is concerned.

—Markel, observed Birck, greatly overestimates the range of his thinking, if he imagines he can consider even the least and weakest of his whiskies and sodas from the angle of eternity. It simply isn't within his power. He'd never come out alive. I seem to remember reading somewhere or other that to do this is God's exclusive prerogative. And that, no doubt, is why He has ceased to exist. . . . The recipe must have been too strong, even for Him.

Markel didn't reply. He looked serious and sad. At least, so it seemed to me, from what I could see of his face there in the darkness, under the great red-striped awning; and as he struck a match to relight his cigar, which had gone out, it suddenly seemed to me he'd grown old. He'll die between forty and fifty, I thought to myself. For the rest, he's well over forty.

Suddenly Birck, who was sitting in such a way that he could look out over the pavement towards the town, said:

—Look, there's Mrs Gregorius coming along. The woman who's married to that disgusting clergyman. God alone knows how she happened to get caught by him. Seeing those two together makes one turn one's head away. The simplest neighbourly consideration requires it.

—Is the Vicar with her? I asked.

—No. She's alone. . . .

Of course. The parson was still at Porla.

—I think she looks like a blonde Delilah, said Birck.

MARKEL: Then let's hope she has a proper understanding for her rôle in life and puts enormous horns on the Nazarite of the Lord.

BIRCK: I should hardly think so. Naturally, she's religious. Nothing else could explain that marriage.

MARKEL: On the contrary, according to my simple notions it would be incomprehensible if, after a suitable period of marriage with the Rev. Gregorius, she had the tiniest inkling of religion left in her—and anyway, she can't possibly be more religious than Madame de Maintenon. The true faith is an invaluable help in all life's predicaments and has never hindered the traffic.

Our talk fell silent as she went by in the direction of the Museum and Skeppsholmen. She was wearing a simple black dress. She walked neither slow nor fast, looked neither right nor left.

Yes, her walk. . . . Involuntarily, as she went by, I had to close my eyes. She has the walk of someone going to her fate. She went with her head lowered a little, so that the nape of her neck shone white under the fair hair. Did she smile? I can't say. But suddenly I chanced to recall my dream of the other night. The sort of smile she wore then, in that horrible dream. I have never seen her smile it in reality; and never wish to.

When I looked up again I saw Klas Recke going by in the same direction. As he passed us he nodded to Birck and Markel; perhaps also to me, it was hard to say. Markel waved to him to come and sit with us, but he passed on, pretending not to notice. He was followin her footsteps. And I thought I saw a strong hand holding them both, the same invisible string, drawing

both of them in the same direction. And I asked myself: Where was the way leading, for her, for him?
But what's that to me! The way she is going she
would have gone without my help. I've merely removed a little of the nastiest dirt out of the way of her
little feet. But her path, even so, is certainly a rough one.
It must be. The world isn't kind to those who love.
And in the end it leads into the darkness, for them and
for all of us.

—Recke's been hard to get hold of recently, Markel
said. I'm certain that rascal's up to something. I've
heard it said he's after a little girl with a lot of money.
Well, well, that's what will happen in the end, he has
the debts of a crown prince. He's in the hands of the
moneylenders.

—How do you know that? I asked, perhaps a shade
more testily than there was any reason for.

—I don't, he replied insolently. I don't know it at
all. But I perceive it. Vulgar minds have a way of
assessing a man by his financial position. I go the other
way about it: I assess the financial situation by the man.
It's more logical. And I know Recke.

—You're not to drink any more whisky, Markel,
Birck said.

Markel poured himself out another whisky, and one
more for Birck, who sat staring into the empty air,
pretending to see nothing. My drink was almost un-
touched, and Markel regarded it with a worried glance
of disfavour.

Suddenly Birck turned to me:

—Tell me, he asked, are you looking for happiness?

—I suppose so, I replied. The only definition of
happiness known to me is: what everyone in his own
situation finds desirable. Therefore it must surely be
self-evident that we are all trying to find it.

Birck: Of course. In that way it's self-evident. And your answer reminds me for the hundredth time that all philosophy lives by, and wholly feeds on, verbal ambiguities. Against the happiness-pancake so ardently desired by the mob, one person sets up his birthday-cake of salvation and another 'his work'; and both deny that they so much as know what is meant by trying to find happiness. An enviable gift this, of being able to deceive oneself with words. Haven't we all, always, a need to see ourselves and our efforts in the light of a certain ideality? Perhaps then in the last resort the deepest happiness lies in the illusion of not desiring happiness.

Markel: Man doesn't pursue happiness, only pleasure. "It's possible," said the Cyrenäics, "that there may be people who don't pursue pleasure; but, if so, the reason is that their intelligence is deformed and their judgment impaired."

—When philosophers, he went on, say that man seeks happiness, or 'salvation', or 'his work', they are only thinking of themselves, or at least of adults enjoying a certain degree of education. In one of his short stories Per Hallström relates how when he was small he used to pray: "The lantern comes, the lantern goes, whom God loves the lantern knows."[1]

Obviously at that tender age he didn't know the meaning of the word 'happiness' and therefore unconsciously replaced this unknown and uncomprehensible word with another, more familiar and easily understood. But the cells in our body know as little about 'happiness' or 'salvation' or a 'work' as infants do. And it's these cells that determine all our strivings. Every-

[1] Swedish *'lyckan'* = happiness, *'lyktan'* = the lantern. An untranslatable verbal equivoce. "Happiness comes, happiness goes; whom God loves, happiness knows"—Swedish child's prayer. *Tr.*

thing on earth that goes under the name of organic life flees from pain and seeks pleasure. Philosophers are only thinking of their own conscious efforts, their *willed* efforts: that's to say, their imaginary efforts. But the unconscious part of our being is a thousandfold greater and mightier than the conscious, and it's the unconscious that tips the balance.

BIRCK: All you've just noted merely confirms my belief in what I said just now, that if we are to talk philosophy to any purpose, language must be re-made from the ground up.

MARKEL: Well, for God's sake, keep your happiness, I'll take the pleasure. Skål! But even if I agree to your way of using words, that doesn't mean it's true that everyone seeks happiness. There are people who haven't any gift for it at all and are painfully and ruthlessly aware of the fact. Such people don't seek happiness, only to get a little form and style into their unhappiness.

And, suddenly without warning, he added:

—Glas is one of them.

This last astounded me. I just sat there, without a word to reply. Right up to the moment I heard my own name uttered I thought he was speaking of himself. And I still think so. It was simply in order to conceal it that he pounced upon me. An oppressive silence followed. I looked out over the glittering waters of The Stream. In the cloud-masses over Rosenbad the moonlight broke through, and a pale silvery light fell on the pillared façade of the old palace of the Bonde family. Over the Mälaren lakes a violet red cloud sailed on its solitary way, detached from the others.

July 25

Helga Gregorius: she is always before my eyes. I see

her as I saw her in my dream: naked, holding out to me
a bunch of dark flowers. Red perhaps, but very dark.
Well, red is always dark in the twilight.

I never go to bed at night without wishing she would
come to me again in my dreams.

But that ambiguous smile my imagination has gradually managed to erase; I see it no longer.

*　　*　　*

I wish the parson was back. Then she would be sure
to come to me again. I want to see her and hear her
voice. I want her close to me.

July 26

The clergyman: his face, too, persecutes me—with
just that expression it wore at our last encounter, when
I began to discuss sexual matters. How can I describe
that expression? It was the expression of someone who
smells something rotten and secretly finds the smell
agreeable.

August 2

The moon is shining. All my windows are open. In
my study the lamp burns. I have put it on my escritoire,
in the lee of the night-breeze which with its gentle hush
fills the curtain like a sail. I walk to and fro in the room,
stopping now and then at my writing-desk and jotting
down a line. For a long while I've been standing at one
of the windows of the sitting-room, looking out and
listening for all the strange sounds that belong to the
night. But tonight silence reigns, down there beneath
the dark trees. Only a solitary woman sits on a bench;
she has been sitting there a long while. And the moon
is shining.

*　　*　　*

When I came home at dinnertime a book was lying on my writing-desk. I opened it. A visiting card fell out: Eva Martens.

I remember she spoke of this book the other day, and I said, à propos of nothing, that it would be fun to read it. I said this out of politeness and in order not to be guilty of the indelicacy of scorning something in which she was interested. Since then I have not thought of the matter again.

But evidently she has.

Is it very stupid of me if I fancy she's just the littlest bit in love with me? I can see it written on her that she is in love. But if she loves someone else, how can she have so much interest over for me?

She has two bright, honest eyes and a wealth of brown hair. The nose is not perfectly modelled. The mouth—I don't remember her mouth. Oh yes, it's red and rather on the large side; but I don't see it clearly before me. And anyhow one is only really familiar with a mouth one has kissed, or longed very much to kiss. I know such a mouth.

I sit looking at the little simple, correct visiting-card, with the name in pale lithographic type. But I see more than the name. There's a sort of writing which only becomes visible under the influence of great warmth. Whether I possess such warmth, I don't know; but I can read the invisible writing even so: "Kiss me, be my husband, give me children, let me love. I am longing to be allowed to love."

"Here go many virgins, whom no man has yet touched, and who do not thrive by sleeping alone. Such shall have good men."

Thus, more or less, spake Zarathustra. The real one, the old one; not the chap with the whip.

Am I a 'good man'? Could I be her good man?

I wonder what image she can have formed of me. In her light heart, which contains only a few gentle and friendly thoughts about those close to her and perhaps a little rubbish besides, an image has formed, having certain outward features that are mine, but which is not me, and in that image, it seems, she is well pleased—God knows why, perhaps chiefly because I am unmarried. But if she really knew me, if by some chance for instance she happened to read what I write on these scraps of paper in the evenings, well then, I fancy she would shun the paths I walk in. I should think the gulf between our souls is a bit too broad. But who knows? When entering marriage it is fortunate, perhaps, if the gulf is as broad as this—if it were narrower, I should perhaps be tempted to try and fill it in, and that would never turn out well! But even so: to live side by side with her and never give her access to that which is truly me and mine—can one treat a woman so? Let her embrace another, believing it to be me—is it permissible to do such a thing?

Well, of course; of course one can! In reality, surely, this is what is always happening: we know so little about one another. We embrace a shadow and love a dream. And, anyway, what do I know about her?

But I'm alone and the moon is shining, and I long for a woman. I could be tempted to go over to the window and call her up, she who is sitting down there alone on the bench, waiting for someone who doesn't come. I have port wine and brandy and beer and good food and the bed has been made.

Wouldn't it be heaven for her?

*　　　*　　　*

I sit thinking of Markel's words the other evening, about myself and happiness. Verily, I might be tempted to marry and be as happy as a sandboy; just to annoy him.

Yes, the moon. There it is again.

I remember so many moons. Oldest of them all is the one that perched behind the windowpanes in my childhood's earliest winter evenings. Always it hovered over a white roof. Once my mother read Viktor Rydberg's *The Christmas Goblin* aloud to us children; I recognised it at once. But it still had none of the characteristics it was later to possess. It was neither wild nor sentimental, nor cold and horrible. It was just big and shiny. It belonged to the window, and the window belonged to the room. It lived in our home.

Later on, after they had noticed I was musical and let me take piano lessons and I'd got as far as being able to strum a little Chopin, then the moon became new for me. One night, I was about twelve then, I remember lying awake, unable to sleep because I had Chopin's Twelfth Nocturne running through my head, and because of the moonlight. We were in the country. We had just moved out there, the room where I lay was still without a blind. The wild white moonlight flooded into my room, over bed and pillow. I sat upright in bed and sang. I had to sing that wonderful wordless melody that I couldn't get away from. It melted into the moonlight and in both lay a promise of something tremendous, something to be my lot one day; I didn't exactly know what, an unhallowed happiness, or an unhappiness worth more than all the happiness in the world, something burning and delightful and grand, awaiting me. And I sang until my father stood in the doorway and yelled at me to go to sleep.

That was Chopin's moon. And it was the same moon

86

which afterwards shivered and burned over the water on August evenings when Alice sang. I loved her.

Then, too, I remember my Uppsala moon. Never have I seen a moon with so cold or averted a face. Uppsala has quite another climate from Stockholm, an inland climate with air drier and clearer. One winter night I was walking to and fro with an older friend on the white snowy streets with their grey houses and black shadows. We talked philosophy. With my seventeen years behind me I scarcely believed in God; but I was being cussed about Darwinism; it made everything seem meaningless, stupid, squalid. We went in beneath a black vaulting and up some stairs and stood close to the cathedral walls. The builder's scaffolding made it seem like the skeleton of some unheard-of monster from the depths of dead strata. My friend spoke of our kinship with our brothers the animals; he talked and proved and shouted with a hoarse uncultivated voice whose provincial accent echoed among the walls. I did not say much in reply, but I thought to myself: You're wrong, but I still haven't studied or thought enough to be able to refute you. But wait—wait just one year, and I'll come back to this same spot with you, in the moonlight, just like it is now, and I'll prove how wrong and stupid you are. For what you say cannot, must not, on any terms whatever, be the truth; if it is true, then I don't want to have any more part in things, I have no business in such a world. But my comrade talked and waved a little German volume he was holding in his hand, and out of which he had got his arguments. Suddenly he stopped in the full light of the moon, opened the book at a place where there were some illustrations to the text and handed it to me. The moon shone so brightly I could both see what it represented and read what was written beneath. It was a picture of three craniums, rather similar: the skulls of an ourang-outang, an Australian aborigine, and of Immanuel Kant. Seized with loathing, I flung the book away from me. My comrade flew into a rage and attacked me; we wrestled and fought in the moonlight, but he was stronger and got me under him and 'washed' my face in the snow, the way schoolboys do.

One year passed, and others too, but I never felt equal to refuting him; it was a job I found better left alone. And though I do not really understand what business I have in this world, still I have stayed in it.

And many moons I have seen since then. A mild and sentimental moon between silver-birches by the lake-side. . . . The moon scurrying through sea-mists . . . the moon fleeing away through ragged autumn clouds . . . the lovers' moon which shone on Gretchen's garden window and Juliet's balcony. . . . A girl no longer young who wanted to get married told me once that she could not help crying whenever she saw the moon shining over a little wooden cottage in the forest . . . the moon is passionate and desirous, says a poet. Another tries to find a tendentious ethical-religious meaning in moonbeams, likening them to threads the dear departed spin into a web to catch errant souls in. For youth the moon is a promise of all those tremendous things which await it, for older people a memento that the promise was never kept, a reminder of all that broke and went to pieces. . . .

And what *is* moonshine?

Secondhand sunshine. Diluted, counterfeit.

The moon just now creeping out from behind the church spire has a face of ill omen. Its features seem to me distorted, dissolute, frayed by a nameless suffering. Wretched man, why are you sitting up there? Are you doomed, a counterfeiter—have you counterfeited the sunshine?

In truth, no mean crime. If one could only be certain of never committing it.

Light!

. . . I sat up in bed and lit the lamp on my bedside table. I had been lying in a cold sweat, my hair stuck to my forehead. What was it I had been dreaming?

Always and always the same thing. That I killed the clergyman. That he had to die because he already smelt of the grave; and it was my duty to do it. . . . I found it difficult, unpleasant. This was something unprecedented in my practice—gladly would I have consulted a colleague, unwilling as I was to bear solitary responsibility in so grave a matter. . . . But far off, Mrs Gregorius was standing naked in a corner, in half-darkness, trying to cover herself with a little black veil. And when she heard me utter the word 'colleague' such a desperate and terrified look came into her eyes I realised it had to be done at once. Otherwise, in some way I could not clearly understand, she was lost; and I must do it alone, in such a way that no one would ever find out. So, my head averted, I did it. How? I don't know. I only know I held my nose and turned my head away, saying to myself: There, there, now it's all over. Now he doesn't smell any more. And I wanted to explain to Mrs Gregorius that it was a very rare and strange case: most people, of course, only smell after they are dead, and then they are buried; but if someone smells while he's still alive, then he has to be killed, the present state of science knows no other way out. . . . But Mrs Gregorius had vanished and all round me was only a great vacuum in which everything seemed to flee away and avoid me.

. . . The darkness lifted, giving way to an ashy moon-light. And I was sitting bolt upright in my bed, wide awake, listening to my own voice. . . .

I got up, put on a few clothes, and lit the lamps in all the rooms. I walked to and fro with clocklike regularity, I don't know how long. At length I stopped in front of the sitting-room mirror and stared at my pale demented self, as if at a stranger. But a fear of yielding to a sudden impulse and smashing to pieces that old mirror which has seen my childhood, almost my whole life, together with much that happened before I existed, assailed me; and I went over and stood at an open window. The moon was no longer shining. It was raining, and the rain blew full into my face. It was a relief.

'Dreams run like streams.' . . . Hoary proverbial wisdom, I know you well. And in reality most of what one dreams is not worth a second thought—loose frag-ments of experience, often the silliest and most in-different, fragments of those things consciousness has judged unworthy of preservation but which, even so, go on living a shadow life of their own in the attics and box-rooms of the mind. But there are other dreams. As a lad I remember sitting a whole afternoon pondering on a geometrical problem, and in the end having to go to bed with it still unsolved: asleep, my brain went on working of its own accord and a dream gave me the solution. And it was correct. Dreams there are, too, like bubbles from the depths. And now I come to think of it more clearly—many a time has a dream taught me something about myself, often revealed to me wishes I did not *wish* to wish, desires of which I did not wish to take daylight cognizance. These wishes, these dreams, I've afterwards weighed and tested in bright sunshine. But rarely have they stood up to the daylight, and more often than not I've flung them back into the foul depths

where they belong. In the night they might assail me
anew, but I recognised them and, even in dreams,
laughed them to scorn, until they relinquished all claim
to arise and live in reality and the light of day.

But this is something else. And I want to know what
it is, weigh it, assess it. One of the basic instincts of my
being, it is, never to suffer in myself anything half-
conscious, half-clear, whenever it lies in my power to
bring it out into the light of day, hold it up, see what
it is.

So, let's think:

A woman came to me in her hour of need and I
promised to help her. Help, yes . . . neither of us, then,
had realised or reflected on what this meant, or might
come to mean. What she requested of me was, after all,
so simple and easy. It cost me neither effort nor qualm
of conscience, indeed it mostly amused me. I did this
lovely woman a delicate service and at the same time
played a nasty trick on that loathsome parson, the whole
episode dropping into my dense black spleen like a rosy
spark from a world closed to me. . . . And, for her, did
it not mean life and happiness—as she saw it and got
me to see it? I promised to help her, and so I did . . .
what had to be done at the time.

But since then the whole thing has gradually come
to wear quite another aspect, and this time I must take
care to search out the heart of the matter before I
proceed.

I promised to help her; but I don't like doing things
by halves. And now, of course, I know and have known
it a long while: she cannot be helped, short of being
set free.

In a day or two the parson will be back—and the old
tale begins all over again. I know him now. But not
merely this; in the last resort she would anyway have

had to get over it by herself, however hard it was, even if it tore her life to pieces and left her a shred. But there's something tells me, as if it had already come to pass, she will soon be bearing a child under her heart. Loving as she now does, there's little chance of her avoiding it. Perhaps she doesn't even want to. And then: if this happens—when it happens—what then . . .? Then the parson must be put away. Right away.

True: if this happens, then it's possible she will come to me and ask me to 'help' her with the same sort of help so many have begged for in vain—and if she does, well then, I suppose I shall have to accede, because I do not see how I can resist her in anything. But that's the end of the matter as far as I'm concerned. I've had enough.

But I feel, I feel and I know, it won't turn out like that. She isn't like the others, she'll never ask me for *that* sort of help.

And so the parson must go.

Turn and twist it as I will, I can see no other solution. Get him to see reason? Make him see he no longer has the right to foul her life, that he must set her free? Nonsense. She's his wife; he's her husband. Everything will be on his side: the world; God; his own conscience. Love, for him, is naturally the same as it was for Luther: a need of Nature, which his god once and for all has given him permission to satisfy with this particular woman. That she meets his desires with frigid distaste can never for a moment make him doubt his 'rights'. Anyway he assumes, I suppose, that at these moments she secretly feels the same as he does, but as far as he's concerned it is perfectly in order that a Christian woman and a clergyman's wife should not admit as much, even to herself. Even for his own part he doesn't really like calling 'all that' a pleasure; he would rather

92

it was called 'a duty' and 'God's will'. . . . No, away with such a creature, away with him, away!

Let me think: I was looking for a feat to perform, wasn't I. Begging for it. Can this, then, be the feat, *my* feat? The thing which has to be done, which I alone see must be done, and which no one except myself can, or dares, do?

One could say it looks a bit strange. But that's no reason, neither for nor against. An action's 'greatness' or 'beauty' is but the reflected light of its effect on the public. But since it is my humble if natural intention to keep the public in every sense out of this affair, this aspect needn't be considered. I am solely concerned with myself. I want to inspect the seams of my action; see what it looks like inside.

First and foremost: do I really seriously want to kill the clergyman?

'Want to'—well, and what does that mean? A human will is no unit; it's a synthesis of hundreds of conflicting impulses. A synthesis is a fiction; the will is a fiction. But we need fictions, and no fiction is more needful to us than the will. Well then: *do you want to?*

I want to; and I don't want to.

I hear conflicting voices. I must interrogate them; I must know *why* the one says: I want to, and the other: I don't want to.

You first, who say 'I want to': Why do you want to? Reply!

—I want to act. Life is action, When I see something that makes me indignant, I want to intervene. If I don't intervene every time I see a fly in a spider's web, this is because the world of flies and spiders is not mine, and I know one must limit oneself; and I don't like flies. But if I see a beautiful little insect with shimmering golden wings caught in a web, then I tear the

93

web to pieces and kill the spider, if need be, for I do not believe it is forbidden to kill spiders. I go walking in the forest; I hear a cry of distress; I run towards the cry and find a man about to rape a woman. Naturally I do what I can to free her, and, if need be, kill the man. The law does not give me the right to do so. The law only gives me the right to kill another in self-defence, and by self-defence the law only means defence when in direct peril of my own life. The law does not let me kill someone else to save my father or my son or my best friend, or to protect my beloved from violence or rape. In a word, the law is absurd; and no self-respecting person allows his actions to be determined by it.

—But the unwritten law? Morality . . .?

—My good friend, the law, you know as well as I do, is in a state of flux. Even during those few fleeting moments the two of us have been living in this world, it has undergone visible changes. Morality, the proverbial line chalked round a hen, binds those who believe in it. Morality, that's others' views of what is right. But what was here in question was my view. True, in many cases, perhaps the vast majority, and in those that occur most often, my view of what is right is in tolerable agreement with others', with 'morality'; and in a multitude of other instances I even find the divergence of view arising between myself and morality is not worth the risks entailed in deviating from it; and therefore submit. Thus morality becomes consciously for me what it is in practice for each and every person, although all do not recognise it: not a fixed law, binding above all, but a *modus vivendi*, useful for daily life in that unremitting state of war which exists between oneself and the world. I know and I concede that current morality in its broad and general outlines expresses, like the bourgeois law, a concept of right and wrong, the fruit of immemorial ages, handed down from generation to generation slowly growing and changing, concerning those conditions most necessary for mankind's social existence. I recognise too that, if life here on earth is to be at all liveable for such creatures as ourselves—creatures not to be conceived within any other frame than that of our social organisation and nurtured by all its changing rights, libraries and museums, police and waterworks, street lamps, nightly garbage disposal, changing of the guard, sermons, opera, ballet, and so forth—these laws, by and large, must be more or less generally respected. But I know, too, that those individuals who have had anything to them have never taken the law pedantically. Morality's place is among household chattels, not among the gods. It is for our use, not our ruler. And it is to be used with discrimination, 'with a little pinch of salt'. For prudence sake we should always adopt the customs of any place we come to, but to adopt them whole-heartedly or with conviction would merely be simple-minded. I'm a traveller in this world; I look at mankind's customs and adopt those I find useful. And morality is derived from '*morales*', custom; it reposes entirely on custom, habit; it knows no other ground. And I don't need to be told that, by killing that parson, I'm committing an action which is not customary. Morality—you're joking!

—I admit I raised the question largely as a matter of form. Where morality is concerned I believe we see eye to eye. But I'm not letting go of you, even so. Initially the question we were discussing was not, in essence, how, flat in the face of custom and morality, you dare to do what we are talking of; it was a question *why* you want to. You replied with a parable, the rapist who outrages a woman in the forest. What a comparison!

On the one hand a crude criminal; on the other a blameless and respectable old clergyman!

—Yes, I admit my comparison limps a little. I referred to an unknown woman and an unknown man and to an imperfectly known relation between them. It isn't at all certain the unknown woman is worth my committing murder for her sake. Nor is it certain this unknown man who thus falls in with a young woman in the depths of the forest and is suddenly possessed and overwhelmed by Pan is, for that reason, worthy of death.

Finally, I cannot be sure such danger really threatens as would make such intervention necessary! The girl screams because she's frightened and because it hurts; but that's not to say the damage is to be measured by her screams. It may well turn out that these two people become friends before parting. Many a country marriage has begun with rape and yet turned out no worse than others and once upon a time the violent abduction of women was the normal form for engagement and marriage. If, therefore, in my chosen example, I kill the man to free the woman—the sort of action I fancy most people of moral views, jurists apart, would approve, and which, before a French or American jury, would even lead to my sensational acquittal, to public applause—I'm acting on pure impulse, without reflection; and it may well be I do something very stupid. But our affair is of quite a different order. Here is no question of an isolated case of rape, but of a relationship which is a matter of life and death and which, in essence, constitutes continuous, repeated rape. Here is no question of some man unknown, of value unknown, but of someone you know only too well! The Reverend Gregorius. Here it's a question of helping and saving, not a woman unknown, but your secret beloved. . . .

—No, no! That's enough! Not a word more!

—Can a man let the woman he loves be outraged, despoiled, trampled on, before his very eyes?

—Be quiet! She loves someone else. This is his business, not mine.

—You know you love her. Therefore it's your business.

—Be quiet! . . . I'm a doctor. And you want me hugger-mugger to murder an old man who comes to me for help!

—You're a doctor. How many times haven't you uttered that expression: Your duty as a doctor. Well, here it is now: perfectly clear, I think. Your duty as a doctor is to help the person who can and should be helped, and cut away the rotten flesh which is spoiling the healthy. Certainly, there's no glory to be reaped: you can't let anyone know of it, or you'll be sitting inside Långholmen or Konradsberg.

Afterwards I recall how a sudden gust of wind blew the curtain against the lamp, how its fringe caught fire and how I instantly stifled the little blue flame in my hand and shut the window. I did these things automatically, almost without being aware of it. The rain lashed the window-pane. The lights burned on, still and stiff. On one of them was a little fragile grey nightmoth.

I sat staring at the stiff flames of the lamps, as if I wasn't there at all. I fancy I sank into a sort of coma. Maybe I slept a while. But suddenly I gave a start, as if from a violent shock, and remembered everything: the question that had to be solved, the decision to be taken, before I could go to rest.

Well, then, you *don't* want to: *why* don't you want to?

—I'm frightened. First and foremost, frightened

of being found out and 'punished'. I don't under-estimate your prudence and thoughtfulness on my behalf, and I can quite believe you will arrange every-thing so that it turns out satisfactorily. I deem it probable. But, even so, the risk is there. Chance. . . . One never knows what can happen.

—One has to risk something in this world. You wanted to act. Have you forgotten what you wrote here in your diary not so many weeks ago, before we knew anything of all that has happened since? Position, re-spectability, future, all these things you were ready to stow aboard the first ship to come sailing by laden with action. . . . Have you forgotten that? Shall I turn up the page?

—No. I haven't forgotten. But it wasn't true! I was bragging. I feel different, now I see the ship coming. Surely you can understand I never imagined it could be such a satanic ghost-ship? I was boasting. I tell you. Lying! No one can hear us; I can be honest. My life is empty, wretched, I see no sense in it; yet I cling to it; I like to walk in the sunshine and observe the crowd. I don't want to have something to hide and be frightened of. Leave me in peace!

—Peace, no—you won't have any peace, anyway. Do you want to see the woman you love drowning in a cesspool, when by one bold swift action I can help her out? Will I have any peace then, can I ever be at peace, if I turn my back on her and go out into the sunshine and look at the crowd? Will that be peace?

—I'm frightened. Not so much that I'll be found out; I've always got my pills and can quit the game if people begin to smell a rat. But I'm scared of myself. What do I know about myself? I'm frightened of get-ting involved in something that binds and entangles me, never lets me go. What you require of me meets with no obstacle in my views; it's an action of which, in anyone else, I should approve providing I knew what I know; but it's not my line of country. It conflicts with my inclinations, habits, instincts, everything that's essentially me. I'm not made for such things, I tell you. There are thousands of brisk, capital fellows who will as soon kill a man as a fly. Why can't one of them do it? I'm afraid of having a bad conscience; for that's what you get if you try to shuffle out of your skin. To behave yourself means to know your limitations; and I want to behave myself.

Every day people commit with the greatest ease and pleasure actions which fly in the face of their deepest and best-founded opinions, and their consciences thrive like little fish in water. But try and act against your own innermost structure, then you'll hear how your conscience screams! Then you'll hear feline music! You say I've been begging and pleading for an action to commit—it's impossible, it simply isn't true, there must be some misunderstanding. It's unthinkable I ever had so insane a wish—I who am a born looker-on, who want to sit comfortably in my box and see how people on the stage murder each other, while I myself have no business there. I want to stay outside. Leave me in peace!

—Trash! You're just trash!

—I'm scared. This is a nightmare. What have I to do with these people and their filthy affairs! The priest is so loathsome to me I'm scared of him—I don't want his fate mixed up with mine. What do I know about him? What I loathe about him isn't 'him', himself, but the impression he has made on me—he has certainly met hundreds and thousands of people without affecting them as he does me. The image he has deposited in my soul can't be wiped out just because he disappears, least of all if he disappears because of me. Already, alive, he has come to obsess me more than I like; who knows what he can get up to when he's dead? I know all about that. I've read Raskolnikov, I've read Thérèse Raquin. I don't believe in ghosts, but I don't want to bring things to such a pass that I shall begin to. What has all this got to do with me? I want to go away. I want to see woods and mountains and rivers. I want to stroll under big green trees with a finely bound little volume in my pocket and think beautiful, fine, benevolent, quiet thoughts, thoughts one can utter out loud and be famous for. Let me go, let me go away tomorrow.

—Trash!

Against the grey light of dawn the lamps burned with a dirty brown flame. On my writing-desk the night-moth lay with scorched wings.

I flung myself on my bed.

August 8

I've been riding and bathing. My morning surgery is over and I've paid my usual visits to my patients. Again evening falls. I am tired.

The brick tower of the church looks so red in the evening sun. The trees' greenery is so grand and dark just now, and the blueness beyond is so deep. It's Saturday evening: poor little children are playing hop-scotch down on the gravel path. At an open window a man sits in his shirtsleeves, playing the flute. He plays the intermezzo from *Cavaleria Rusticana*. Strange, how melodies catch on! Scarcely ten years ago this tune arose out of chaos and crept over an impoverished Italian musician, perhaps one evening in the twilight, perhaps just such an evening as this. Inseminating his soul, it gave birth to other melodies, other rhythms and

in consort with them instantly made him world-famous;
gave him a new life, with new happiness, new sorrows,
and a fortune to throw away at the tables at Monte
Carlo. So the melody spreads out like a disease all
round the earth, doing its fated deed for good or ill,
bringing a blush to cheeks and making eyes sparkle;
is admired and loved by countless numbers, or in
others, often those who at first loved it most, awakens
only disgust and boredom. Ruthless, obstinate, it rings
in the ears of those who cannot sleep at nights; infuri-
ates the businessman who lies fretting because the
shares he sold last week have gone up; pains and disturbs the thinker trying to collect his thoughts to
formulate a new law, or dances about in the empty
spaces of an idiot's brain. And all the while, as the man
who 'created' it, perhaps more than any other, is
sickened and plagued by it, it calls forth salvoes of
applause evening after evening from the public in every
place of entertainment on earth; and the man over
there plays it with feeling on his flute.

August 9

To will is to be able to choose. Oh, that it should be
so hard to choose!

Choice is self-denial. Oh, that self-denial should
be so hard!

A little prince was about to make an excursion. They
asked him: Will Your Highness go on horseback or by
boat? He answered: I want to ride on horseback and
take the boat.

We want to have everything, want to be everything.
We want to know all the pleasures of happiness, and
every depth of suffering. We want the pathos of action
and the peace of the onlooker. We desire both the
desert's stillness and the uproar of the forum. At

once we wish to be the thoughts of the thinker and the voice of the crowd; we want to be both melody and harmony. At once! How can such a thing be possible!

"I want to ride on horseback and take the boat."

August 10

There's something flattened and empty about a watch without hands. It's reminiscent of a dead man's face. I am sitting looking at such a watch. In point of fact it isn't a watch at all, but an empty case with a beautiful old watch-face to it. Just now I saw it in the window of the hunchback watchmaker in the alley as I was coming home through the hot yellow twilight—a strange twilight; I've imagined such ends to days in the desert. . . . I went in and asked the watchmaker, who has mended my watch for me once, what sort of a watch it was, that had no hands. He threw me a coquettish hunchback's smile and showed me the lovely old silver case, a fine piece of work; he had bought the watch at an auction, but the works were worn out, useless, and his intention had been to put in some new ones. I bought the case as it was.

My intention is to put some of my pills inside it and carry it in my righthand waistcoat pocket as an appendage to my watch. A variant, only, to Demosthenes' idea of poison in a pen. There's nothing new under the sun!

*   *   *

Now night falls; already a star is winking through the foliage of the big chestnut tree. I have a feeling I shall sleep well tonight; it is cool and calm inside my head. Yet I find it hard to drag myself away from the tree and the star.

Night. Such a lovely word! Night is older than day, said the ancient Gauls. They believed the brief transient day was born of endless night.

The great, endless night.

Well, that's but a manner of speaking of course. . . . What is night, what is it we call the night? The slender conical shadow of our little planet. A little pointed cone of darkness in the midst of a sea of light. And this sea of light? what is it? A spark in space. The tiny effulgence around a little star: the sun.

Ah, what sort of a plague is this, that has seized on mankind, making them ask what everything is? What sort of a scourge is it, whipping them out of the family circle of their creeping and walking and running and climbing and flying brethren, here on earth; driving them out, to see their world and their life from above, from outside, with cold estranged eyes, and find it little, and nothing worth? Where are we going? Where will it all end? I must think of the woman's voice I heard complaining in my dream; I still hear it in my ears, the voice of an old woman, grown old with weeping: The world's on fire, the world's on fire!

Look at your world from your own point of view, not from some point in space. Modestly measure with your own yardstick, after your own status, your own predicament, the status and the predicament of man the earthdweller. Then life is large enough and a thing of consequence; and night endless, deep.

August 12

So gorgeously the sun shines on the weather-cock this evening!

I am fond of this lovely intelligent creature who always turns with the wind. To me he is a standing reminder of the cock who on a certain occasion crowed thrice, and an ingenious symbol of holy church, who is always denying her master.

In the churchyard the shepherd of the parish strolls slowly to and fro in the beautiful summer evening, supporting himself on the arm of a younger colleague. My window is open and outside it's so still that a word or two of what they are saying reaches up to me. They are talking of the imminent election of a new archbishop, and I heard the rector mention the name Gregorius. He pronounced the name without enthusiasm and with not entirely unmixed sympathies. Gregorius is one of those clergymen who have always had the laity on their side and therefore their own colleagues against them. From his tone of voice I gathered that the rector mentioned his name more or less in passing, he did not regard him as having any serious chances.

This is also my view. I do not think he has a chance. I should be much surprised if he became Archbishop...

Today is the twelfth of August; he went to Porla on the fourth or fifth of July and was to stay there for six weeks. Therefore it will not be many days before we have him here again, in health and spirits after his visit to the waters.

August 13

How is it to be done? I have known a long while now. Chance has so arranged matters that the solution is as good as given: my potassium cyanide pills which I once made up without a thought to anyone but myself, must be brought into service.

One thing is self-evident: there can be no question of letting him swallow them at home. It must happen here, at my place. It won't be nice, but I see no alternative, and I want to bring this matter to a head. If he takes a pill at home, on my prescription, and is promptly done for, it's to be feared the police might tumble to a connection between these two facts. What is worse, she whom I wish to save might easily be suspected and drawn into the affair, her name sullied for life, perhaps condemned for murder. . . .

Obviously nothing must occur which might arouse the police. No one must know the parson has been given a pill. He must die a perfectly natural death, from heart attack. Nor must *she* suspect anything else. For him to die in my surgery is naturally rather bad for my reputation as a doctor and will give my witty friends stuff for unpleasant comment: but that must make no odds.

One day he comes up to me, talks about his heart or some other nonsense and wants me to certify that he is better after his bathing cure. No one hears what we are talking about; the big empty sitting-room lies between the waiting-room and my surgery. I listen, tap, declare a remarkable improvement; but say there is, even so, one thing which worries me a little. . . . I take out my pills, explain they are a new drug against certain cardiac ailments (I shall have to think up some name or other), and advise him to take it at once. I offer him a glass of port to wash it down with. Does he drink wine? Of course, I have heard him cite the wedding at Cana. . . . He shall have a nice little wine. Grönstedt's Grey Label. I can see him in front of me; first he sips the wine, then he puts the pill on his tongue, drains the glass and washes it down. His spectacles reflect the window and hide his glance . . . I turn away, go over to the window and look out over the churchyard, stand drumming my fingers on the window-pane . . . he says something, that it was a nice wine, for example, but stops in mid-sentence . . . I hear a thud . . . he's lying on the floor. . . .

But if he refuses to take his pill? Oh yes, he'll take it as a delicacy, he's crazy about medicine . . . but *if*? Well, I can't help it, the matter must drop. After all, I can't kill him with an axe.

. . . He's lying on the floor. I remove the pill-box, the bottle of wine, the glass. I ring for Kristin. The Vicar's ill, a fainting attack, it'll soon pass over . . . I feel his pulse, his heart:

—It's a stroke, I say at last. He's dead.

I ring up a colleague. Well now—who? Let me think. *He* won't do; seven years ago he wrote a thesis which I reviewed a bit sceptically in a medical journal. *Him*; too much sense. Him and him and him: gone away. *Him*—yes, we'll have to take him. Or else him; or, if need be, him.

I show myself in the doorway of my waiting-room, probably just about as pale as I ought to be, and declare in a low controlled voice that something has happened which obliges me to break off my surgery hour for today.

My colleague arrives. I explain what has happened. The Vicar had long been suffering from severe heart-trouble. In a friendly way he condoles with me on my wretched bad luck that the demise should have occurred just here, in my room, and at my request writes out a death certificate. . . . No, I won't give the clergyman any wine; he might spill it on himself, or the smell might give away the fact he has been drinking it, and that may be a troublesome thing to explain. . . . He'll have to be content with a glass of water. Anyway I'm of the opinion that wine is deleterious.

But what if it comes to an autopsy? Well, then I shall have to take a pill myself.

It is an illusion to suppose one can get embroiled in an undertaking of this sort without running a risk, so much I have known from the outset. I must be prepared for drastic developments.

Strictly, of course, the situation requires that I myself call for an autopsy. I don't see anyone else doing it—well, one can never be sure. . . . I tell my colleague I intend to ask for an autopsy; presumably he replies that it isn't really necessary, objectively speaking, the cause of death being obvious; but for form's sake it might be the right thing, after all. Afterwards I let the matter drop. Here, anyway, is a flaw in my plan. I shall have to give it some closer thought.

Impossible, for the rest, to arrange every detail in advance. Chance will make its changes, even so. One must rely to some small degree on one's powers of improvisation.

Another thing—hell and damnation, what a fool I am! There isn't only myself to think of. Suppose it really does come to an autopsy and I swallow a pill and vanish through my trap-door to keep Gregorius company crossing the Styx, what explanation will be found for so rare a crime? Won't people turn for an explanation to the living—to *her*? Drag her before a court, examine her, bully her. . . . That she has a lover, will soon be sniffed out. That she must have desired the priest's death, longed for it to happen, would be almost self-evident. So much she might not even bother to deny. Everything turns black before my eyes. . . . And it would have been I who brought you to this pass, loveliest of blooms and of women!

I worry myself blind and grey over this.

But perhaps—perhaps I have an idea, even so. If I see an autopsy is necessary, then, in good time, before I take my pills, I must show clear symptoms of insanity. Still better—the one, indeed, does not exclude the other—I'll write a document which I shall leave lying open here on my desk in this room where I shall die; a paper scribbled all over with raving nonsense indicating persecution mania, religious *idées fixes*, and so forth. For years the priest has been persecuting me. He has poisoned my soul, therefore I have now poisoned his body. I have acted in self-defence, etc. Some biblical qoutations can also be woven in, there are always a few that will suit. In this way light will be thrown on the affair. The murderer was crazy. That's explanation enough, no need to look for any other. I am given Christian burial and Kristin receives confirmation of what she has always secretly suspected—well, not always so secretly, either. She has told me a hundred times I am out of my mind. If need be, she can witness on my behalf.

August 14

I wish I had a friend to confide in. A friend to consult. But I have no one, and even if I did—after all there are limits to what one can ask of one's friends.

Always, I have been rather solitary. My loneliness I have borne about with me through the crowd as a snail his house. For some individuals solitude isn't a circumstance they've tumbled into by chance, but a trait, of character. And this, I suppose, can only deepen my solitude. Whatever happens, whether things turn out well or ill—for me the 'punishment' can only be solitary confinement for life.

August 17

Fool! Trash! Cretin!
But, what's the use of invective—no one can prevail over his nerves and stomach.

My surgery was over long ago. The last patient had just gone. I was standing at my sitting-room window, thinking of nothing, when suddenly I see Gregorius walking diagonally across the churchyard, straight for my doorway. Everything turned grey and misty. I hadn't expected him, didn't know he was back. I felt giddy, dizzy, sick, all the symptoms of sea-sickness. I had but one thought in my head: not now, not now! Another time, not now! He's coming up the stairs, he's standing outside my door, what am I to do. . . . Out to Kristin: If anyone asks for me, tell them I'm out. . . . From her wide eyes and gaping mouth I realised I looked strange. Rushing into my bedroom, I locked the door. I only just reached the handbasin in time: then I vomited.

*   *   *

So, my fear was right? I'm not up to it!
For it was just now it should have happened. He who wants to act must seize his chance. No one knows whether it will ever come back. I'm not up to it!

August 21

Today I've seen her and talked to her.
I walked out to Skeppsholmen in the afternoon. Just across the bridge I met Recke: he was coming down from the hill where the church is. He walked slowly, looking at the ground, underlip thrust out, knocking pebbles out of his way with his stick. He didn't seem exactly pleased with his existence. I thought he wouldn't see me; but just as we passed each other he looked up and nodded in a gay and hearty manner there was no mistaking, his whole face changing expression. I went on my way, but halted after a few steps. She can't be far away, I thought. Perhaps she's still up there on the

hill. They've had something to say to each other and have had a rendez-vous up there where hardly anyone ever goes; and so as not to be seen with him she has let him go down first. I sat down on the bench which surrounds the poplar, and waited. I should think it must be the biggest tree in Stockholm. Many a spring evening in my childhood have I sat beneath this tree with my mother. Father never came; he didn't like taking walks with us.

No, she didn't come. I thought I should see her coming down from the hill, but perhaps she had gone down another way, or had never been there at all.

Anyway, I went up the hill by a roundabout path, past the church—and there I saw her, sitting crouched on one of the steps outside the church door, leaning forward, chin in hand. She sat looking straight into the sun, which was just then setting. That was why she did not immediately notice me.

The very first time I ever saw her it struck me how unlike all others she is. She isn't like a woman of the world, or a middle-class wife, or a woman of the people. Mostly the last, perhaps; particularly as she sat there, just then, on the church steps, with her fair hair free and bared to the sun, for she had taken off her hat and laid it beside her. But a woman from a primitive folk, or one that never existed, where class distinctions had not yet begun, where 'the people' still had not become the lower classes. A daughter of a free tribe.

Suddenly I saw she was weeping. Not with sobs, only tears. Crying like one who has wept much and hardly notices she is doing it.

I wanted to turn back and go away, but at the same moment I realised she had seen me. I saluted her a little stiffly, made to walk past. But at once she got up from the low step, as lightly and softly as from a chair,

and coming forward put out her hand. Hastily she
dried her tears, put her hat on and drew a grey veil
over her face.

We stood silent awhile.

—It's lovely up here this evening, I said at last.

—Yes, she said, it's a lovely evening. And it has
been a lovely summer. Now it will soon be over. The
trees are already turning yellow. Look, a swallow!

A solitary swallow flitted past us, so close that I felt
the air fanned cold on my eyelids. It curved sharply,
its course seeming to the eye to make an angle acute
as an arrowhead, and then vanished into the blue.

—The heat came so early this year, she said. That
usually means an early autumn.

—How is the Vicar? I asked.

—Thank you, she replied. Quite well. He came
home from Porla a couple of days ago.

—And is he at all better?

She averted her head a little, screwing up her eyes
as she looked into the sunlight.

—Not from my point of view, he isn't, she replied
in a low voice.

I understood. Just as I had expected. Well, it was
not exactly hard to guess. . . .

An old woman was sweeping up withered leaves.
She came closer and closer to us, and slowly we walked
out of her way, further out on to the hillside. As I
walked I thought of the clergyman. First I had scared
him with his wife's health; that had worked for hardly
two weeks. Then I had scared him with his own, and
grim death; and that had worked for six. And, if it had
worked for so long, then only because he had been
separated from her. I begin to think Markel and his
Cyrenäics are right: people care nothing for happiness,
they look only for pleasure. They seek pleasure even

flat in the face of their own interests, their own opinions, their faith, their happiness. . . . And the young woman who was walking beside me so straight and proud, though her neck with all its fair silken tresses was bowed deep beneath worries—she had done exactly the same: sought pleasure, caring nothing for happiness. And now it struck me for the first time how it was precisely the same behaviour which, while it filled me with disgust for the old clergyman, inspired in me an endless sympathy for the young woman, yes, with a shy awe as in the presence of the godhead.

Through the thick cloud of dust over the town the sun shone less brilliantly now.

—Tell me, Mrs Gregorius,—may I ask you a question?

—Please do.

—The man you love—I don't even know who he is—what does he say about all this, and the whole business? What does he want to do? What does he want to come of it? Surely he can't be satisfied with things as they are—?

A long silence. I began to think I had asked something stupid and that she did not wish to answer.

—He wants to take me away, she said at length.

I started.

—And *can* he? I asked. I mean, is he a free man, well-to-do, independent of employment or profession, a man who can do as he likes?

—No. Or we should have done it long ago. He has his whole future here. But he wants to make a new way for himself in a foreign country, far away. Perhaps America.

I had to smile within myself. Klas Recke and America! But when I thought of her I felt cold. I thought: over there, thanks to precisely those same qualities that keep him afloat here, he'll go straight to the bottom. And then what will become of her?

I asked.:

—And you yourself—do *you* want to go?

She shook her head. Her eyes filled with tears.

—I mostly want to die, she said.

Gradually the sun drowned in the grey mist. A chill breeze sighed through the trees.

—I don't want to ruin his life. Be a burden to him. Why should he go away? It would only be for my sake. His whole life is here, position, future, friends, everything.

There was nothing I could reply to this, she was only too right. And I thought of Recke. Such a suggestion, coming from him, seemed to me so strange. I should never have expected such a thing of him.

—Tell me, Mrs Gregorius—you regard me as your friend, don't you? Therefore I can be your friend. You don't dislike me talking to you about these things?

She smiled at me through her tears and veil, yes, she smiled!

—I'm very fond of you, she said. You've done something for me which no one else could or would have done. You may talk to me about anything you wish. I like it so much when you talk.

—Has he, your friend, has he wanted it for a long time, for you to go away together? Has he been talking about it long?

—Never before this evening. We met up here shortly before you came. He has never spoken to me about it before.

I began to understand. I asked:

—Does that mean something has happened just now . . . since he has hit on this idea? Something worrying?

She bowed her head:

—Perhaps.

Again the old woman with the broom was sweeping up her leaves close to us; we went back toward the church, slowly, in silence. We stopped by the steps where we had first met. She was tired: she sat down again on the step, and put her chin in her hand, gazing out into the grey falling dusk.

Neither of us spoke for a long while. Everything around us was still, but over our heads the wind soughed through the treetops with a sharper tone than before, and there was no more warmth in the air.

She shivered.

—I want to die, she said. I should so terribly like to die. I feel I have had everything that is mine, all I was meant to have. Never again can I be so happy as I've been these weeks. There has seldom been a day when I haven't wept; but I've been happy. I regret nothing, but I want to die. Yet it's so difficult. I think suicide is ugly, particularly for a woman. I do so loathe any violence to nature. And I don't want to bring him any sorrow, either.

I was silent and let her speak. She screwed up her eyes.

—Yes, suicide is ugly. But it can be even uglier to go on living. It's terrible how often one's only choice is between that which is more or less ugly. If I could only die!

—I'm not afraid of death. Even if I believed there was anything after death I wouldn't be frightened of it. Nothing I have done, either good or evil, could I have done otherwise; I've done what I had to do, in big things as in small. Do you remember how I once talked to you of my first love, and said I regretted not giving myself to him? I don't regret it any longer. I don't regret anything, not even my marriage. Nothing could have happened otherwise than it has.

—But I don't believe there is anything after death. As a child I always imagined the soul as a little bird. In an illustrated history of the world belonging to my father I saw how the Egyptians, also, depicted it as a bird. But a bird flies no higher than there is air, and that isn't far. It, too, belongs to earth. In school we had a natural history teacher who told us how nothing of what exists on earth can ever leave it.

—I'm afraid he got that a bit mixed up, I interposed.

—It's possible. Anyway, I gave up my bird-faith, and the soul became vaguer to me. Some years ago I read everything I could lay my hands on about religion, both for and against. Of course it helped me to clear my mind on a number of matters, but I never learned what I wanted to know. There are people who write so extraordinarily well, I believe they can prove anything. I always thought the one who wrote best and most beautifully was right. I worshipped Viktor Rydberg. But I felt and understood that, on the subject of life and death, no one knew anything.

A high warm colour came into her cheek in the dusk.

—But latterly I've come to know more about myself than in my whole life before. I've learned to feel and understand that my body is me. There is no joy, no sorrow, no life at all, except through it. And my body knows very well it must die. It feels it, as an animal can feel it. And that is how I now know there is nothing for me on the other side of death.

It has grown dark. The buzz of the city came up to us more strangely in the darkness, and down there at the corners of quays and bridges the lamps began to be lit.

—Yes, I said, your body knows it will one day have to die. But it doesn't *want* to die; it wants to live. It doesn't want to die until it's worn out and burdened with years. Consumed by suffering and burned up by pleasure. Then, and not until then, will it want to die. You think you want to die because everything looks so bleak just now. But you don't really want it, I know you can't want it. Let time go by. Take each day as it comes. Sooner than you realise, everything can change completely. You, too, can change. You are strong and healthy; you can be stronger still; you are one of those who can grow and be renewed.

A shiver passed through her form. She got up:

—It's late. I must go home. We can't go down from here together, it wouldn't do for anyone to see us. Go that way, and I'll go in the other direction. Goodnight!

She gave me her hand. I said:

—I should so like to kiss your cheek? May I?

She lifted her veil and proffered her cheek. I kissed it. She said:

—I want to kiss your forehead. It is beautiful.

The wind tugged at my thinning hairs as I bared my head. And she took it between her warm soft hands and kissed my brow—ceremoniously, as if in a rite.

August 22

What a morning! A faint feeling of autumn in the glass-clear air. And still.

Met Miss Mertens on my morning ride and exchanged a few gay words with her as we passed. I like her eyes. I think there's more depth in them than one sees at first. And then her hair. . . . But after that there's not so much to add to the list of her merits. Oh yes, without question she has a good little character too.

I rode round Djurgården thinking all the while of her who had sat on the steps up there by the church and looked into the sun and wept, and who longed to die. And in truth: if no help comes, if nothing occurs—if that which I am thinking does not occur—then any attempt to help her with words is only silly chatter; this much I felt, even as I was speaking to her. Then she would be right, right a hundred times over, to seek death. She can neither go away nor stay. Go away—with Klas Recke? Be a burden to him, a ball chained to his leg? I bless her for not wanting to. They would both go under. He is nicely off here, so they say, with one foot in his department of the Civil Service and the other in finance. I have even heard people call him a man with a future, and if he has debts, well, things are no worse for him than they are for many other 'men with futures' before their position is made. He has just that amount of talent which usually helps a man on—in the right environment, of course; an elemental force he certainly is not. 'Make his own way' ... no, that's not his line at all. No more can she go on living her old life. A prisoner in enemy territory. Bear her child under a strange man's roof and be obliged to play the hypocrite and lie to him and see his disgusting paternal joy—diluted, it may be, with suspicions he dare not voice but which he will make use of in order still further to poison her life. No, she quite simply *cannot do it*; if she tries, it will end with some catastrophe. ... She must be free. She must be on her own, free to decide over herself and her child, as she may wish. Then everything will turn out well for her, life will become possible and good for her to live. I have sworn an oath on my soul: she shall be free.

During my surgery hour just now, I was in a horrible state of tension. I thought he would come today, I seemed to feel it in my bones. ... He did not come, but that's all one; whenever he comes, he will not find me unprepared. What happened last Thursday is not to be repeated.

Now I am going out to have dinner. I should like to meet Markel, then I could invite him to dine with me at Hasselbacken. I want to talk, drink wine, see people.

Kristin has already got my dinner ready and she will be livid; but it's all one.

(Later)

It's over. It's done. I've done it.

So queerly it came about. So strangely did chance arrange it for me. I might almost be tempted to believe in providence.

I feel light, empty, like a blown egg. As I came in through the sitting-room door just now and saw myself in the mirror the expression on my face made me start. There was something empty, flat, about it; something, I don't know what, reminding me of the handless watch I carry about with me in my pocket. And I had to ask myself: What you've done today—is that all there has been inside you, is nothing left?

Foolishness. A feeling that will go over. I'm a little tired in my head. So much I may be allowed.

It's half-past seven; the sun has just set. It was a quarter-past four when I went out. Three hours, that is . . . three hours and a few minutes.

. . . Well, I went out to have dinner somewhere; I cut obliquely across the churchyard; walked through the alley; stopped a moment outside the watchmaker's window, was greeted with an ingratiating hunchback grin from the man inside, and replied to it, making, I remember, this reflection: Every time I see a hunchback, sympathy makes me feel something of a hunchback myself. Presumably a reflexual effect of that sympathy with misfortune drummed into us in childhood. . . . I came out into Drottninggatan; went into the Havana Store and bought two good Uppmanns; turned the corner into Fredsgatan. Entering Gustaf Adolf's Square I threw a glance into the window of Rydberg's, just in case Markel happened to be sitting there over his absinthe, as he sometimes does. But only Birck sat there in front of a glass of lemonade. A bore; I didn't feel the least inclination to have dinner with him tête à tête.

Outside the newspaper office I bought an *Aftonblad* and stuck it in my pocket. Maybe there's something new in it about the Dreyfus Affair, I thought . . . but all the while, as I went on walking, I was wondering how I could lay my hands on Markel. No use ringing up his office, he's never there at that time; and as I thought this I went into a tobacconist's and telephoned. He had just gone out. . . . On Jakob Square, then, far off, I saw the Rev. Gregorius coming towards me. I was making ready to salute him, when all of a sudden I discovered it was not him at all. There was not even any particular resemblance.

—So, I thought to myself, I'll meet him soon, then.

For according to popular belief, which I recalled my own experience had confirmed on some occasion, to mistake a person in this way is a sort of intimation. I even remembered having read in a pseudo-scientific journal 'for psychic research' a story about a man who, after such a 'warning', turned sharply into a sidestreet in order to avoid a disagreeable encounter—and ran straight into the arms of the very person he was seeking to avoid. . . . But I do not believe in such nonsense, and all the while my thoughts were still engaged in this razzia after Markel. It occurred to me I had once or twice met him at this time of day by the lemonade kiosk on the market-place. So I went there. Naturally, he was not to be seen, but anyway I sat down on one of the benches beneath the great trees by the church wall to drink a glass of Vichy water while I glanced through my *Aftonblad*. Hardly had I unfolded it and fastened my eyes on the standing bold-type headlines: The Dreyfus Affair—when I heard heavy crunching steps on the gravel, and the Rev. Gregorius stood before me.

—Well now, if it isn't you, Doctor. How are you, how are you. May I sit down? I was just going to drink a glass of vichy water before dinner. Surely that can't be bad for the heart, can it?

—Well, I replied, carbon dioxide isn't good, of course, but a little glass now and then can't do you much harm. How do you feel after your visit to the baths?

—Very fit. It was just what I needed, I think. I paid you a visit a few days ago, Doctor, Thursday I think it must have been, but I came too late. You'd gone out.

I replied that more often than not I am available for half-an-hour or so after my surgery hour is over; but that day I had unfortunately been obliged to go out a little earlier than usual. I asked him to come tomorrow. He was not sure he had time, but he would try.

—It's beautiful at Porla, he said.

(It is very ugly at Porla. But Gregorius, a townsman, habitually finds 'the country' beautiful, whatever it looks like. What was more, he had paid for it and wanted to get the last drop of value for his money. So he found it beautiful.)

—Yes, I replied, it's quite nice at Porla. Though less beautiful than most other places.

—Perhaps Ronneby is more beautiful, he conceded. But it's such a long and expensive journey.

A half-grown girl served our vichy water, two small quarter bottles.

Suddenly I had an inspiration. Since it had got to happen,—why not here? I looked about me. No one was near us just then. At a table far away sat three old gentlemen, one of whom, a retired cavalry captain, was known to me; but they were talking loudly together, telling tales and laughing, and so were not able to hear what we said or did.

A dirty little barefoot girl came padding up to us, proffering us flowers. We shook our heads and she silently vanished. Before us spread the gravel spaces of the square, almost empty at this late afternoon hour. Now and then, from the corner by the church, a pedestrian would take a short-cut down to the eastern avenue. A warm late summer sun gilded the Dramatic Theatre's old yellow façade between the linden trees. On the pavement the manager of the theatre was standing talking to the producer. The distance reduced them to miniatures, the play of their outlines only to be grasped and interpreted by an eye already familiar with them. The producer was betrayed by his red fez, which gleamed like a little spark in the sunshine, and the manager by those delicate movements of his hands which seemed to say: Well, damn it all, there are two sides to everything! I felt sure he was saying something of the sort. I saw the slight shrug of his shoulders, even seemed to hear his tone of voice. And I applied the words to my own affairs. Yes, there are two sides to everything. But no matter how wide you open your eyes to both of them, in the end you are obliged to choose only one. And I had long ago made my choice.

From my waistcoat pocket I took out the watchcase with the pills, selected a pill between my thumb and forefinger, turned aside slightly, and pretended to take it. Then I drank a gulp of water out of my glass, as if to wash it down. The clergyman was at once interested:

—I believe you're taking medicine, Doctor? he said.

—Yes, I replied. We've bad hearts, both of us. Mine isn't all it ought to be, either. Comes from smoking too much. If only I could give up smoking, I'd never need this rubbish; it's quite a new drug. I've seen it highly recommended in German medical journals, but I felt I ought to try it out myself before using it in my practice. I've been taking it for more than a month now, and find it excellent. You take one pill shortly before dinner; it hinders 'food fever', the distress and palpitations that immediately follow a meal. May I?

I proffered him the little box. Its lid was open, and turned in such a way he could not see it was a watch-face; that would only have given him stuff for unnecessary questions and chatter.

—Thank you, thank you, he said.

—I can write out a prescription for them tomorrow, I added.

Without further questions he took a pill, and swallowed it down with a draught of water. I thought my heart would stand still. I stared straight ahead of me. The square lay empty, dry as a desert. A majestic police constable walked slowly past, stopped, flicked a grain of dust off his well-brushed overcoat, and went on along his beat. The sun still shone as warm and yellow on the wall of the Dramatic Theatre, as before. Now the manager made a gesture he uses but rarely, the Jewish gesture of out-turned hands, the business-man's gesture meaning: I turn it inside out, I hide nothing, I put my cards on the table. And the red fez nodded twice.

—This lemonade stall is an old one, the clergyman said. It must be the oldest of its sort in Stockholm.

—Yes, I replied, without turning my head. It's old.

The clock on Jakob's Church struck thrice. A quarter to five.

Mechanically I took out my watch to see if it was keeping good time; but I fumbled, and my hand shook so that I dropped it on the ground, smashing the glass. Bending down to pick it up again I saw a pill lying on the ground; it was the one I had just pretended to take. As I crushed it beneath my foot, I heard the clergyman's tumbler fall over on the tray. I did not want to look, yet I saw his arm fall limply down and his head nod on his breast and the senseless eyes wide open. . . .

Ridiculous, but that was the third time since I came home I've got up and made sure my door is properly shut. What have I to fear? Nothing. Not the least thing! I have done my business, neatly and delicately, whatever else might be said about it. Chance, too, helped me. It was lucky I saw the pill lying on the ground and trod it to pieces. If I had not dropped my watch, I suppose I should never have seen it. So it was lucky I dropped my watch. . . .

The parson is dead, of a heart attack; I myself wrote out the death certificate. Hot and breathless from walking in the strong summer heat, and altogether too violently and without waiting for it to settle, he drank a big glass of vichy water. This I explained to the majestic police constable, who had turned and come back; to the terrified little waitress; and to a few curious persons who had gathered. I had advised the clergyman to wait a little, let the fizziness go out of his vichy water before he drank it; but he was thirsty and wouldn't listen. "Yes", said the constable, "as I went by just now I saw how violently and thirstily the old gentleman drank his water. And I thought: that isn't good for him. . . ." Among the passers-by who stopped was a young curate, who knew the deceased. He undertook to inform Mrs Gregorius, as gently as possible.

I've nothing to fear. Why, then, do I keep on feeling my door? Because I sense the enormous atmospheric pressure of others' opinions; the living, the dead, and the still unborn, gathering out there, threatening to blow down the door and crush me, pulverize me . . . that's why I try the lock.

At last, when I got away, I climbed up on to a tram, the first I could get hold of. It took me far out on to Kungsholmen. I went on by road as far as the Traneberg Bridge. We lived there once, one summer, when I was four or five years old. It was there I caught my first perch on a bent pin. I remembered the precise spot where I stood. Again I stood there a long while, inhaling the familiar smell of stagnant water and sundried tar. Now, as then, swift little perch darted hither and thither under the water. I remembered how greedily I had looked at them, and how hot my longing had been to catch them. And when at last I succeeded, and a tiny, tiny perch, hardly three inches long, was squirming on my hook, I screamed with delight and ran straight home to Mamma with the little fish hopping and shivering in my clutched hand. . . . I wanted us to eat it for dinner; but Mamma gave it to the cat. That was fun, too. To see how he played with it and then to hear the bones crunching between his fierce teeth. . . .

On my way home I went into the Piperska Muren to have dinner. I did not expect to meet anyone I knew, but three doctors were sitting there and they waved to me to come and join them. I drank a glass of pilsner and left.

What am I to do with these pieces of paper? My habit hitherto has been to lay them in the secret drawer of my chiffonier; but this is no good. An eye of the least experience immediately perceives that such an old piece of furniture must have a secret drawer, and easily finds it out. If, in spite of all, something should happen, something not to have been foreseen, and anyone should hit on the idea of ransacking my home, they would soon be discovered.

But how am I to get rid of them? I know: I have a lot of cardboard boxes on my bookshelf, cases shaped like books, filled with scientific jottings and other old papers, carefully arranged in order and with labels on their backs. I'll have them in among my notes on gynaecology. And I can mingle them with sheets from my older diaries. for I have kept a diary before; never regularly, never for long, but periodically. . . . Anyhow, for the time being it's all one. I shall always have time to burn them, if need be.

*　　　*　　　*

It's over. I'm free. Now I shall shake this off, and think of something else.

Yes—but what?

I'm tired and empty. I feel absolutely empty. Like a punctured boil.

The simple fact is, I'm hungry. Kristin will have to heat up my dinner and bring it in.

August 23

All night it has been raining and blowing. Autumn's first storm. I lay awake listening to two boughs of the great chestnut tree outside my window creaking against each other. I remember I got up and sat by the window awhile, watching the ragged clouds chase one another across the sky. In the reflected gaslight they took on a dirty, fiery, brick-red glow. The church spire seemed to be bending to the storm. The clouds took on the shapes of dirty red devils blowing horns and whistling and screeching in wild pursuit as they whipped the rags off each other's bodies in all sorts of whoredom. And as I sat there I suddenly burst out laughing: I laughed at the storm. I thought I was taking the whole affair altogether too seriously. I was acting like the Jew when lightning struck just as he was eating a pork chop; he thought it was for the chop's sake. I was thinking of myself and my affairs; therefore I fancied the storm did the same. At length I dropped off to sleep in my chair. A cold shiver woke me. I went back to bed, but not to sleep. So at length a new day dawned.

A still grey morning, now; but it rains and rains. And I have a terrible cold in the nose. Already I've drenched three handkerchiefs.

Opening the newspaper over my morning coffee, I saw that the Rev. Gregorious was dead. Quite suddenly, a stroke. . . . by the lemonade stall in Kungst#rädgården Park . . . one of the better-known doctors, who chanced to be in his company, could only confirm that death had occurred. The deceased was one of the capital's most popular preachers . . . had the ear of the public . . . an agreeable and open-hearted personality . . . fifty-eight years old . . . mourned by a wife, *née* Waller, and an aged mother.

Ah well, for God's sake, that's the way we must all go. And his heart had long been weak.

But he had an old mother, did he? I didn't know that. She must be frightfully old.

There's something grim and unpleasant, I see, about this room, particularly on these rainy days. Everything here is old and dark and moth-eaten. But I don't feel at home with new furniture. At all events I think I shall have to get some new curtains for the window, these are too dark and heavy and keep the light out. One of them is scorched along its edge since that night last summer when the lamp flickered and it caught fire.

"That night last summer. . . ." Let me think, how long ago can that be? Two weeks. And to me it seems a whole eternity.

Who could have guessed he had his mother still alive. . . .

How old would my mother have been now, if she had lived? Oh, not so terribly old, at that. Hardly sixty.

She would have had white hair. Perhaps she would find hills and stairs rather heavy going. Age would have made the blue eyes, lighter than everyone else's, still lighter now, and they would smile cheerfully under her white hair. She would have been happy that things have turned out so well for me, but even more would she have mourned for my brother Ernst, who is in Australia and never writes. She never had anything but sorrow and worry over Ernst. That's why she liked him best—But who knows, she might have changed into something else if she had lived.

She died too early, my mother.

But it's a good thing she's dead.

(Later)

Just now, as I came home in the twilight, I stood on the threshold of the sitting-room, petrified. On the table in front of the mirror stood a bunch of dark flowers in a vase. It was dusk. They filled the room with their heavy scent.

They were roses. Dark, red roses. Two were almost black.

In my room, immense in the twilight, I stood stock still, hardly daring to move, hardly breathing. I thought I was walking in a dream. The flowers by the mirror—surely they were the flowers from my dream?

For a moment I was afraid. I thought: this is a hallucination; I'm beginning to go to pieces, this is the beginning of the end. I dared not go over and take the flowers in my hand for fear of grasping empty air. Instead, I went into my study. On the desk lay a letter. With trembling fingers I broke the envelope, thinking it might have some connection with the flowers; but it was only an invitation to dinner. I read it and wrote a word in reply on a visiting card: 'Coming'. Then I went out into the sitting-room again: the flowers were still there. I rang for Kristin; I wanted to ask her who had brought these flowers. But no one answered the bell. Kristin had gone out. No one was in the flat except myself.

My life is beginning to merge into my dreams. To keep life and dream apart is beginning to be too much for me. I know all about that, I've read about it in big books: it's the beginning of the end. But anyway the end must come one day and there's nothing I'm afraid of. My life becomes more and more a dream. And perhaps it has never been anything else. Perhaps I've been dreaming the whole time, dreamt I'm a doctor and my name is Glas and that there was a parson who was called Gregorius. And at any moment I can wake up and find I'm a street-cleaner or a bishop or a school-boy or a dog—how should I know. . . .?

What nonsense. When dreams and premonitions begin to come true and it isn't a question of servant-maids and old women but more highly organised individuals, then psychiatry says it is a sign of incipient psychic disintegration. But how explain it? The explanation is that in the great majority of cases one has never dreamed what 'comes true'; we *think* we have dreamed it or that we have gone through precisely the same thing before, even to the minutest detail. But my dream with the dark flowers I have written down! And the flowers themselves, they are no hallucination, they stand there, alive, I can smell them, and someone has come here with them.

But who? There's only one person I can guess at. Does this mean she has *understood*? Understood, approved, and sent me these flowers as a sign and an acknowledgment? But that's mad, it's impossible! Such a thing simply doesn't happen, can't be allowed to happen. It would be too awful. Such a thing simply cannot be allowed. There are limits to what a woman may be permitted to understand! If it is so, then I don't understand anything any more, I don't want any further part in this game. Yet they are lovely flowers.

Shall I put them on my writing-desk? No. They can stay where they are. I don't want to touch them. I'm afraid of them. I'm afraid.

August 24

My cold turned into quite a little bout of influenza. I've closed my doors to my patients, so as not to infect them, and I keep indoors. I've told Rubins I'm coming to dinner. I can do nothing, not even read. Just now I was playing patience with an old pack of cards left by my father. I believe there are as many as a dozen old packs of cards in the drawer of the delightful mahogany card-table, a piece of furniture which alone could send me to perdition, if I had the least thirst for play.

As one opens it, the table-top is covered with green

baize; it has long grooves along the edge for the markers, and the most delicate inlay.

Well, that was just about all he did leave me, my good father.

Rain, rain. . . . And it isn't raining water, but dirt. The atmosphere is no longer grey, it's brown. And when, sometimes, the rain falls less heavily awhile, it lightens to a dirty yellow.

On the top of the patience cards on my table lie the scattered leaves of a rose. Why have I been pulling off its petals? I cannot say. Perhaps because I happened to recall how, as children, we once used to throw rose petals into a mortar and roll them into beads, which we thereafter threaded on to bits of string and gave to Mamma as a necklace for her birthday. They smelt so nice, those beads. But after a few days they shrivelled up like raisins and had to be thrown away.

The roses—well, there was a tale, too! The first thing I saw when I went out into the sitting-room this morning was a visiting-card, lying on the mirror table beside the flower vase: Eva Mertens. To this very moment I do not understand how I could have failed to see it yesterday. And how at the very furthest corner of hell could it have entered the head of that nice pretty girl to send flowers to me, unworthy sinner? By straining my perspicacity, and overcoming my modesty, I can certainly make a guess at the deeper reason; but the immediate cause? Her pretext? However much I ponder the matter I can think of no other reason than this: She has read or heard tell how I happened to be present on the sad occasion of the clergyman's death; she supposes I am deeply shaken and therefore wishes to send me this evidence of her sympathy. She has acted suddenly, impulsively and as seemed most natural to her. That girl has a good heart. . . .

Supposing I let her love me? I am so lonely. Last winter I had a grey-striped cat, but he ran away at the first approach of spring. Now, as the glow of my first autumn fire dances on the flame-red mat, I remember him; just there, in front of the stove, he used to lie purring. In vain I strove to win his affection. He lapped up my milk and warmed himself by my fire, but his heart remained cold. What became of you, Puss? You had bad blood in you. I fear you'll have gone to pot— that's if you're alive at all. Last night I heard a cat screech in the churchyard, and I was sure I recognised your voice.

*   *   *

Who was it said: "Life is short, but hours are long." It should have been a mathematician like Pascal, but wasn't it Fénélon? Pity it wasn't me.

*   *   *

Why did I thirst for action? Most, perhaps, to cure my boredom. "*L'ennui commun à toute créature bien née*," as Queen Margot of Navarre put it. But it's a long time now since tedium was the privilege of 'persons of birth'. Judging by myself and a few others known to me, it rather looks as though with the rise in enlightenment and welfare it's well on the way to spreading throughout the populace.

Action came to me as a great strange cloud, flung its lightning, and passed over. And tedium remained.

Anyway this is the most damnable influenza weather. On days like these a smell of old corpses seems to me to rise from the churchyard and force its way in through walls and windows. The rain drips on the window-sill. I feel as if it were dripping on my heart, to hollow it out. There's something wrong with my brain. I don't know whether it's too bad, or too good; but certainly it isn't what it ought to be. To make up for it, I feel my heart, at least, is in the right place. Drip—drip—drip. Why are the two little trees by Bellman's grave so thin and wretched? They must be diseased, I think. Perhaps poisoned by gas. He should be sleeping beneath great sighing trees, old Carl Michael. Sleep, yes—are we allowed to sleep? Soundly? If one only knew—two lines from a famous poem come into my head:

> *L'ombre d'un vieux poète erre dans la gouttière*
> *Avec la triste voix d'un fantôme frileux.*

"The shade of an old poet wanders in the roof-gutters, its voice sad as a frozen ghost's." Luckily for Baudelaire, he never had to hear what it sounds like in Swedish. Altogether, it is a damnable language we've got. The words trample on each other's toes and jostle one another in the gutter. And everything so crude and tangible! No half-tones, no airy allusions or soft transitions. A language which seems to have been created to suit the mob's ineradicable habit of blurting out the truth in all weathers.

It becomes darker and darker: December darkness in August. The black rose petals are already shrivelled. But in all this greyness the cards shine on my table, crude laughing colours to remind me how they were once invented to dissipate the melancholia of a sick and crazy prince. But the mere thought of the work involved in collecting them, turning them right side up and shuffling them into another game of patience, makes me mad, and I can only sit looking at them and hearing how "The Knave of Hearts and the Queen of Spades whisper grimly of their buried loves", as the same sonnet says:

> *Le beau valet de coeur et la dame de picque*
> *Causent sinistrement de leurs amours défunts*

I could wish to go over to the filthy old hovel, in the corner there, and drink stout with the girls. Smoke a sour pipe and take a spade with the madame and give her some good advice on her rheumatism. Fat and blooming, she was here last week, bewailing her lot. Under her double chin she wore a thick gold brooch, and paid cash with a five kronor note. A return visit would flatter her.

A ring at the hall door. Now Kristin opens. . . . What can it be? Haven't I said I'm not receiving anyone today . . . a detective? . . . pretending to be ill, in the guise of a patient. . . . Come in, my dear fellow, I'll put you to rights. . . .

Kristin half opened the door and flung a letter with black borders on to my table. Invitation to attend the funeral. . . .

* * *

—My deed, yes. . . . "If Monsieur wishes to have that History in heroic verse, it will cost him 8 skilling. . . ."

August 25

In a dream I saw figures from my youth. I saw her whom I kissed one midsummer night long ago, when I was young, and hadn't killed anyone. Other young girls I saw, too, who belonged to our circle in those days; one who was being prepared for confirmation the year I took my student exam and who was always wanting to talk to me about religion; another, older than I, who was only too willing to stand whispering with me in our garden in the twilight behind a jasmine hedge. And another who always made a fool of me, but who, when I made a fool of her for a change, became furiously angry and went into convulsions of weeping. . . . Pale, they walked in a pale twilight, their eyes wide open and terrified, making signs to each other when I approached I wanted to speak to them, but they turned away and wouldn't answer me. In my dream I thought: It's quite natural. I've changed so, they don't recognise me. But at the same time I realised I was deceiving myself, and that they recognised me only too well.

Waking, I burst into tears.

August 26

Today was the funeral, in Jakob's Church.

I went; I wanted to see her. I wanted to see whether I could catch a spark from her starry eyes, through the veil. But she sat bowed deep beneath her widow's weeds, and didn't lift her eyelids.

The officiating clergyman spoke on Syrak's words: "From morning until evening the time changeth and all things are speedy before the Lord." He has the reputation of being a child of this world. And it's true I've often seen his pate gleaming in the stalls of theatres, and his white hands forming themselves into discreet applause. But he is a prominent rhetorician of the spirit, and it was clear that he, too, was deeply moved by the old words which through inconceivable generations have rung out on occasions of sudden death and hastily opened graves, and which so vividly express the terror felt by the children of men under the unknown hand that casts its shadow over their world, as enigmatically sending them day as night, and life and death. "Immobility, permanence are not given unto us," the clergyman was saying. "It would not be good for us, not possible for us, no, nor even bearable. The law of change belongs not only to death: first and foremost it is the law of life. Yet again we stand here, no less amazed, no less shuddering at change, when suddenly we see it accomplished, and in a way so different from anything we had ever expected. . . . It should not be so, my brethren. We should reflect: The Lord knew the fruit was ripe, although to us it did not seem so, and He has let it fall into His hand. . . ." I felt my eyes becoming moist, and hid my emotion in my hat. At that moment I almost forgot what I knew of the reasons why the fruit had so hastily ripened and fallen . . . or, to be more exact, I felt at root I knew no more about it than anyone else did. All I knew were a few of the most immediate reasons and circumstances, but behind these the long chain of causation lost itself in darkness. I felt my 'action' to be a link in a chain, a wave in a greater movement; a chain and a movement which had had their beginning long before my first thought, long before the day when my father first looked with desire upon my mother. I felt the law of *necessity*: felt it bodily, as a shiver passing through marrow and bone. I felt no guilt. There is no guilt. The shiver I felt was the same as I sometimes feel from great and serious music, or very solitary and elevated thoughts.

It was many years since I had been in a church. I recalled how, as a boy of fourteen or fifteen, I had sat in these same pews, grinding my teeth with fury at the fat scoundrel in his get-up at the altar, and thinking to myself how all this humbug perhaps might last yet another twenty, or at most thirty, years. Once, during a long dreary sermon, I decided to become a clergyman myself. It seemed to me the clergy I had seen and heard were mere bunglers at their job, and that I could do all this far better myself. I should rise, become a bishop, archbishop. And, once an archbishop—by jove, then people would hear some funny sermons! Then there would be crowds in Uppsala Cathedral! But before the clergyman had got to his Amen my story was already over: I had a close friend at school with whom I used to discuss everything; I was in love with a girl; and then, too, I had my mother. To become a bishop I should have had to have lied and pretended to them, too; and that was impossible. A few people, there must always be, one can be honest with. . . . O Lord, that time, that innocent time. . . .

Strange it is to sit and let one's thoughts carry one back to a mood and a mental world of long ago. Thus one feels the flight of time. The law of change, the preacher was saying, (he's got that out of some play by Ibsen, by the bye). It is like seeing an old photograph of oneself. And I thought, too: how long a time can be left me still to wander about at random in this world of enigmas and dreams and phenomena that elude interpretation? Twenty years, maybe; maybe more . . .? If by some ghostly means I had been able at sixteen to see in a vision my life as it is now, how would I have felt? —Who am I in twenty years, in ten? What shall I think, then, of my life today? These days I have been expecting a visit from the Furies. They haven't put in an appearance. I don't believe such things exist. But, who knows—Perhaps they are in no hurry. Perhaps they think they have plenty of time. Who knows what, given a few years, they can do to me?—Who am I in ten years?

So, as the ceremony moved to an end, my thoughts like butterflies fluttered about me. The church doors were thrown open, people jostled at the exit under a din of bells, and under the portals the coffin staggered and swayed like a ship at sea, and a fresh autumn breeze struck me. Outside, a greyish sky and thin pale sunshine. I, too, felt greyish, thin, and pale, as one does after sitting a long while squeezed inside a church, particularly at a funeral or holy communion. I went to the bath house in Malmtorgsgatan, to take a Finnish bath.

When I had undressed, and entered the *bastu*, I heard a well-known voice:

—It's as hot and jolly in here as in a little departmental office of hell. Stina! Brushing in three minutes!

It was Markel. He sat crouched on a shelf, right up under the ceiling, imperfectly hiding his gnawed-off bones behind a fresh *Aftonblad*.

—Don't look at me, he said, as he caught sight of me. Priests and journalists shalt thou not see naked, saith the preacher.

I wound a wet towel round my head and stretched myself out on a shelf.

—À propos of priests, he went on, I see the Rev. Gregorius was buried today. You were at the church, perhaps?

—Yes, I've just come from there.

—I was on duty at the office when the news of his death came in. The man who brought in the copy had made up a long sensational story with your name all mixed up in it. Which, I thought, was unnecessary. I know you don't care much for publicity. I rewrote the lot and crossed out most of it. As you know, our paper represents an enlightened sector of public opinion and we don't make much fuss about a clergyman having a stroke. Though, of course, a few kind words have to be said, and they cost me no great pains. . . . 'Agreeable' came of its own accord, naturally; but it wasn't enough. So it occurred to me he probably had a fatty heart or something of that sort, since he died of a stroke. And my portrait was finished: an agreeable and open-hearted personality.

—My dear friend, I said, yours is a beautiful calling.

—Yes, and that's nothing for you to laugh at, he

replied. Let me tell you something: there are three sorts of people—thinkers, scribblers, and cattle. It is true I secretly count almost all who are called thinkers and poets among the scribblers, and most of the scribblers belong among the cattle. But that's not the point. The business of thinkers is to search out the truth. There is, however, a secret about truth which, oddly enough, is but little known, although I should have thought it was clear as daylight—and it is this: truth is like the sun, its value depends wholly upon our being at a correct distance away from it. If the thinkers were allowed to have everything their own way they would steer our globe straight into the sun and burn us all to ashes. Small wonder, then, their activity sometimes causes the cattle to become restive and bellow: Put out the sun, in the name of Satan, put it out! It's the business of us scribblers to preserve a correct and satisfactory distance from the truth. A really good scribbler—and there aren't many!—*understands* with the thinker, and *feels* with the cattle. It's our job to protect the thinkers from the rage of the cattle and the cattle from too hefty doses of truth. But I admit the latter duty is the easier of the two, and the one we make the best job of in the ordinary way of things; and I admit, too, that in this we have the invaluable help of a mass of spurious thinkers, as well as of the more sensible among the cattle. . . .

—My dear Markel, I replied, you speak wise words, and quite apart from the suspicion, which dawns on me, that you reckon me neither among the thinkers nor the scribblers, but as one of the third species, it would be a real pleasure for me to dine with you. On that unfortunate day when I met the clergyman by the lemonade stall, I had been running all over town looking for you with just this in mind. Can you get free today? If so we'll drive out to Hasselbacken . . .?

—Excellent idea, replied Markel. An idea which alone suffices to class you among the ranks of the thinkers. There are thinkers, I forgot to mention, of such refinement that they hide themselves among the cattle. They are the genteelest sort of all, and I have always regarded you as being one of them. What time? All right, six o'clock, that's perfect.

I went home to free myself of my black trousers and white scarf. At home a pleasant surprise awaited me: my new dark grey suit which I ordered last week was ready and delivered. A blue waistcoat with white spots also forms part of it. It would be hard to achieve a more perfect confection for a Hasselbacken dinner on a fine day in late summer. On the other hand I was worried about Markel's appearance. For in this respect he is completely unpredictable, one day he can be turned out like a diplomat and the next like a tramp—after all, he knows all sorts of people and is as accustomed to move about in public as at home in his rooms. My anxiety was due neither to vanity nor to fear of others: I am a known man; I have my position; and I can dine at Hasselbacken with a hackney coachman if it amuses me; and as for Markel, I always feel honoured by his company without thinking of his clothes. But it wounds my sense of beauty to see a careless turn-out at a beautifully laid table in an elegant restaurant. It can take away at least half my pleasure. There are bigshots who like to underline their grandeur by going about dressed like junk merchants: this is indecent.

I had made my rendez-vous with Markel by Tornberg's clock. I felt pleasant and free, rejuvenated, renewed, as if I had recovered from an illness. The fresh autumn air seemed spiced with the scent of my youthful years. Perhaps this could be traced to the cigarette I was smoking. I had got in a sort which used to delight me in times gone by, but which I had not smoked for many years. . . .

I found Markel in a sparkling good humour, with a scarf resembling a scaly green snakeskin and, in general, so rigged out that Solomon in all his glory was not nearly as chic as he. We got into a cab, the cabby cracked his whip, gave a flick to stimulate both himself and his horse, and drove off.

Markel had greater authority in the place than I, so I had asked him to telephone and make sure of a table for us near the rail of the verandah. While we made up our programme we dallied over an aquavit, a couple of sardines and some salted olives: Potage à la chasseur, fillet of plaice, quails, fruit. Chablis: Mumm extra dry; Manzanilla.

—So you didn't come out to Rubin's on Thursday? asked Markel. Our hostess certainly missed you. She said you have such a nice way of remaining silent.

—I had a cold. Quite impossible. Sat at home and played patience all the morning, and around dinner-time I went to bed. What sort of people were there?

—Oh, a whole menagerie. Birck, among others. He's managed to shed his tapeworm. Rubin told us how it happened: some while ago Birck reached a solemn decision to let his civil service job go to the devil, and devote himself wholly to literature. And when his tapeworm got wind of it, the wise beast also made a decision, and took itself off to another market.

—Well, and does he mean it seriously? I mean Birck? —Not he! He's quite content to have made his decision, and stay in the Customs and Excise. And now he's trying to make out it was only a *ruse de guerre*. . . .

At a far-off table I fancied I glimpsed the face of Klas

140

Recke. Yes, it was really he. In a *partie carrée* with another gentleman and two ladies. I knew none of them.

—Who are these people over there Recke is sitting with? I asked Markel.

He turned, but could not catch sight either of Recke or his company. The noise around us grew, competing with the orchestra, which was intoning the Boulanger March. Markel's face darkened. He is an impassioned Dréyfusard and in this musical number he fancied he perceived an anti-Dreyfus demonstration, put on by a clique of lieutenants.

—Klas Recke? he resumed. I can't see him. But he must be out play-acting with his future in-laws. He'll soon sail into port, I should think. A girl with money has cast her really rather pretty eyes on him. But, à propos pretty eyes, I was sitting beside a certain young Miss Mertens at dinner at Rubin's. A nice girl, really charming. I've never seen her there before. I don't recall how it came about, but I happened to mention your name, and as soon as she realised we were close friends she couldn't talk about anything else and began asking me all sorts of things I didn't know the answers to. . . . Then, suddenly, she fell silent and the lobes of her ears turned scarlet. As far as I can see she's in love with you.

—You're a bit hasty in your conclusions, I objected.

But I reflected on his remarks about Recke, not knowing what to believe. Markel talks so much, without there being anything in it. It's his one weakness. And I didn't like to ask. But he was still talking about Miss Mertens, and spoke so heatedly I felt obliged to jest:

—Obviously you're in love with her yourself. It's

burning a hole in your waistcoat! Take her, my dear Markel, I shan't be a dangerous rival. Me you can easily oust.

He shook his head. He was serious and pale.

—I'm out of the running, he replied.

I said nothing and we fell silent. The waiter served the champagne with the gravity of an acolyte. The orchestra began the Overture to Löhengrin. The rain clouds of the day now passing had blown over, massing themselves in rosy streaks along the horizon; but overhead the empyrean had deepened to infinite depths of blue, blue as this wonderful blue music. I listened to it, and forgot myself. The thoughts and ponderings of recent weeks and the deed in which they had culminated now seemed to me to be floating away into the blue distance, like something already gone, already unreal, something secreted and detached, never to trouble me any more. I knew I should never again wish or be able to do such a thing. Did this mean it had all been a mistake? After all, I had acted as best I knew how. I had weighed and tested, for and against. I had plumbed the matter to the bottom. Had I made a mistake? It was all one, now. At that moment the secret leit-motif broke through in the orchestra: "Thou shalt not ask!" And in this mystical sequence of notes, and these four words, I fancied I descried a sudden revelation of an ancient and secret wisdom. "Thou shalt not ask!" Not go to the bottom of things: or you yourself will go to the bottom. Not seek truth: you won't find it, only lose yourself. "Thou shalt not ask!" The little quantum of truth that is any use to you, you receive gratis and for nothing; and if it is mixed with lies and errors, this too is for your health's sake; undiluted, it would sear your entrails. Don't try to purge your soul of lies, so much else you didn't think of will follow in their wake; you'll only lose yourself, and all that's dear to you. "Thou shalt not ask!"

—When we went to get a subsidy for the Opera out of the Riksdag, said Markel, we have to dun it into their heads that music has an 'ennobling influence'. I wrote some such nonsense myself in a leader last year. Of course, it's true, in a way, although translated into a language comprehensible to our legislators. In the original it would read: Music excites and strengthens, it heightens and confirms. Confirms the pious in his innocuousness, the warrior in his courage, the debauchee in his vices. Bishop Ambrosius banned chromatic progressions in church music since, in his own experience, they gave rise to unchaste fantasies. In the 1730's there was a clergyman at Halle who saw in Handel's music a clear confirmation of the Augsburg Confession. I have the book myself. And out of a motif from Parsifal a good Wagnerian constructs a whole view of life.

We had reached the coffee. I offered Markel my cigar-case. He took a cigar, and gazed at it attentively.

—This cigar has a serious countenance, he said. It must be a good one. Otherwise, I was a bit worried over the cigar question. As a doctor you must know that the good cigars are the most poisonous. Therefore I was anxious you might give me some damned rubbish.

—My dear friend, I replied. From a hygenic point of view the whole of this dinner mocks common sense. In what concerns the cigar, it belongs to an esoteric strain in the tobacco industry. Its appeal is to the elect.

Around us the public had begun to thin out, the electric lighting was turned up and, outside, darkness began to fall.

—Yes, said Markel suddenly, now I see Recke. I can see him in the mirror. And sure enough he's in the company of the lady I surmised. I don't know the others.

—Well, and who is she?

—Miss Lewinson, daughter of the stockbroker who died last year . . . she has half a million.

—And you think he's going to marry for money?

—Why, certainly not! Klas Recke is a man of breeding and sensibility. Calm yourself. You can be sure he will first of all arrange to fall passionately in love with her, and then marry for love. All this he will manage so well, the money will come to him almost as a surprise.

—You know her?

—I've met her, once or twice. She looks very nice. The nose is a shade too sharp, perhaps, and the intellect too. A young woman who with an impeccable sense of probity trims her sails between Spencer and Nietsche, and says "There and there *he* is right, but there and there the other one has hit the bullseye"—such a woman disturbs me, but not in the right way. . . . What did you say?

I hadn't said anything. I sat lost in thought, but my lips, it may be, had moved with my thoughts; perhaps without knowing it I had mumbled something to myself. I saw her before me, she who is ever in my thoughts. I saw her walking to and fro in an empty street at dusk, waiting for someone who did not come. And I mumbled to myself:—Dear one, this is your affair. All this you must go through alone. No one can help you here, and even if I could, I should not wish to. Here you must be strong. And I thought further: It's a good thing you're free and on your own, now. That way you will come through it more easily.

—No, Glas, we can't go on like this, said Markel, distressed. How long do you imagine we're going to sit here without a drop of whisky?

I rang for the waiter and ordered whisky and a pair of rugs, for it was beginning to be chilly. Recke and his party got up and passed our table without seeing us. Indeed he saw nothing at all. He walked with the purposeful gait of a man who aims steadily at a goal. A chair lay slightly in his path. Not noticing it, he knocked it over. All around us the restaurant was empty. An autumn wind sighed in the trees. The dusk grew greyer, denser. Draped in our rugs like red mantles we sat on a long while, talking of matters both low and sublime; and Markel said things which are too true to be affixed with signs upon paper, and which I have forgotten.

August 27

Another day gone, and again it is night and I am sitting at my window.

Lonely one, beloved one!

Do you know already? Do you suffer? Do you stare with waking eyes into the night? Do you writhe in anxiety on your bed?

Do you weep? Or have you no more tears?

But perhaps he is fooling her up to the very end. He is considerate. He remembers she is in mourning for her husband. As yet he has not let her suspect anything. She sleeps soundly, knowing nothing.

Dearest, you must be strong when it comes. You must get over it. You will see how much life still has in store for you.

You must be strong.

September 4

The days come and go, one like another.

And immorality, that flourishes still, I note. Today, for a change, it was a man who wanted me to help his girl-friend out of a fix. He talked about old memories and headmaster Snuffe in Ladugårdslandet.

I was unshakable. I recited my doctor's oath to him. This impressed him to the extent of his offering me two hundred crowns cash, and a bill to the same amount, together with his lifelong friendship. It was almost touching; he seemed to be rather badly off.

I threw him out.

September 7

From dark to dark.

Life, I do not understand you. Sometimes I feel a spiritual giddiness, whispering and warning and muttering that I have gone astray. I felt like this just now. I took out my *procès verbal* of the trial: the papers of my diary where I cross-examine both my interior voices: the one that was willing, and the one that was unwilling. I read it over and over again, and couldn't come to any conclusion, other than that the voice I finally obeyed was the one with the right ring to it, and that it was the other which was hollow. The latter was perhaps the wiser, but I should have lost my last ounce of self-respect if I had obeyed it.

And yet—and yet . . .

I have begun to dream of the priest. This of course was to be expected, and therefore it does not surprise me. I thought I should escape it precisely because I had foreseen it.

*　　　*　　　*

I understand King Herod's distaste for prophets who went about waking up the dead. In other respects he held them in high regard. But this branch of their activities met with his disapproval. . . .

*　　　*　　　*

Life, I do not understand you. But I am not saying it is your fault. I deem it more probable that I am an unnatural son, than that you are an unworthy mother.

And at long last the suspicion begins to dawn on me—perhaps we aren't intended to understand life? All this rage to explain and understand, all this chasing after truth, perhaps it's a wrong turning? We bless the sun because we are living exactly at that distance from it which is healthy for us. A few million miles nearer or further away, and we should burn up or freeze to death. What if it's the same with truth as with the sun?

The old Finnish myth says: He who sees God's face must die.

And Oedipus. He solved the enigma of the Sphinx, and became the unhappiest of mortals.

Not guess at riddles! Not ask! Not think! Thought is an acid, eating us away. At first we imagine it will only eat into that which is rotten and sick and must be removed. But thought thinks otherwise. It eats blindly. It begins with the prey you most gladly throw to it—but don't imagine it will be content with that! It doesn't stop until it has gnawed away the last thing you hold dear.

Perhaps I ought not to have thought so much; perhaps I should have gone on with my studies. 'The sciences are useful because they prevent men from thinking.' It was a scientist who said that. Perhaps I, too, should have lived out my life, as it is called, or 'lived it up', as it is also called. I ought to have gone skiing, kicked a football, lived healthily and gaily with women and friends. I should have married, put children into the world. I ought to have *done* my duty. Such things become footholds, supports. Perhaps, too, it has been stupid of me not to have thrown myself into politics or appeared at elections. The fatherland also makes its demands on us. Well, perhaps there will still be time for that. . . .

The first commandment: Thou shalt not understand too much.

But he who understands that commandment—has already understood too much.

I rave, everything goes round and round.

September 9

I never see her.

Often I go out awhile to Skeppsholmen, merely because it was there I last spoke with her. This evening I stood on the heights by the church and watched the sun set. It struck me how beautiful Stockholm is. I hadn't thought so much about it before. One is always reading in the newspapers that Stockholm is beautiful, so one attaches no importance to it.

September 20

At dinner at Mrs P's today Recke's imminent engagement was spoken of as a known thing.

I become steadily more impossible in company. I forget to answer when people speak to me. Often I don't even hear. I wonder if my sense of hearing is beginning to fail?

And then, these masks! They all wear masks. Worst of all, it is their chief merit. I shouldn't like to see them without. No, nor show myself without! Not to them!

To whom, then?

I left as early as I could. I walked homewards, becoming frozen; suddenly the nights have grown cold. I think a cold winter is on the way.

I walked on, thinking of her. I recalled the first time she came to me and asked for my help. How she suddenly bared herself and revealed her secret, quite unnecessarily. How warmly her cheek burned that day! I remember I said: such things must be kept secret. And she: I *wanted* to say it. I wanted you to know who I am. Supposing I now go to her with my need, as she once came to me? Go to her and say: It is more than I can stand, alone, knowing who I am, wearing a mask, always, for everyone! I must reveal myself to one other person; *one* other must know who I am. . . .

Oh, we should both go out of our minds.

I wandered at random through the streets. I came to the house where she lives. A light was shining in one of her windows. No blind was drawn; she needs none, for on the other side of the street there are only large unbuilt sites with timber yards, and no one can look in. Nor did I see anything, no dark figure, no arm or hand moving, only yellow lamplight on the muslin curtains. I thought: what is she doing now, what occupies her? Is she reading a book, or sitting with her head in her hands, thinking; or doing her hair for the night. . . . Oh, if I were there, if I could be with her . . . lie there and look at her and wait, while she does her hair in front of the mirror and slowly undoes her clothes. . . . But not as at the beginning, a first time, but as one time among many, in a good habit, long enjoyed. Everything that has a beginning must also have an end. This should have neither beginning nor end.

I do not know how long I stood there motionless as a statue. A swollen cloudy sky, faintly irridiscent with moonlight, moved slowly above my head, like a remote landscape. I was cold. The street was empty. I saw a street-walker coming out of the darkness, approaching. Halfway past me she stopped, turned, and looked at me with hungry eyes. I shook my head: so she went away, melting into the darkness.

Suddenly, in the lock of the door, I heard a key rattle. It opened and a dark form glided out. Was it really she? Going out in the middle of the night, without snuffing her lamp? . . . What is this? I thought my heart would stop. I wanted to see where she was going. Slowly, I followed.

She only went to the letter-box at the corner, threw a letter into it and hurried quickly back. I saw her face under a street lamp: it was pale as wax.

I do not know whether she saw me.

*　　*　　*

Never will she be mine; never. I never brought a flush to her cheek, and it is not I who now have made it so chalk-white. And never will she slip across the street in the night, with anxiety in her heart and a letter to me.

Life has passed me by.

October 7

Autumn pillages my trees. Already the chestnut outside my window is naked and black. Clouds fly in thick droves over the rooftops, and I never see the sun.

I have got new curtains for my study; pure white. When I awoke this morning I thought at first it had been snowing. In my room the light was exactly as it is after a first fall of snow. I even fancied I caught the scent of snow freshly fallen. And soon it will come, the snow. One feels it in the air.

It will be welcome. Let it come. Let it fall.

Printed in the United States
by Baker & Taylor Publisher Services